Vampire Kisses 8

Cryptic Cravings

PRAISE FOR

Vampire Kisses

An ALA Quick Pick for Reluctant Young Adult Readers
A New York Public Library Book for the Teen Age

"All in all, a good read for those who want a vampire
love story without the gore." —*School Library Journal*

"As in her *Teenage Mermaid*, Schreiber adds some refreshing
twists to genre archetypes and modern-day stereotypes."
—*Publishers Weekly*

"Horror hooks such as a haunted mansion, a romantic
teenage vampire, and a dark heroine who wins against the
golden guys make this a title that readers will bite into with
Goth gusto." —*The Bulletin of the Center for Children's Books*

"Schreiber uses a careful balance of humor, irony, pathos,
and romance as she develops a plot that introduces the
possibility of a real vampire." —ALA *Booklist*

Kissing Coffins
Vampire Kisses 2

"Raven is exactly the kind of girl a Goth can look up to."
—*Morbid Outlook* magazine

"Readers will love this funny novel with bite!"
—*Wow* magazine

Vampireville
Vampire Kisses 3

"A fun, fast read for vampire fans."—*School Library Journal*

Dance with a Vampire
Vampire Kisses 4

"This novel, like the first three, is never short on laughs and shudders. Alexander is as romantic as ever, and Raven is still delightfully earthy. Schreiber again concocts a lively and suspenseful story that ends on a tantalizing cliffhanger. Fans of the series will be anxious to find out whether Raven's relationship with Alexander will survive." —*VOYA*

"A good choice for Goth lovers and fans of romantic vampire stories."
—*School Library Journal*

Also by Ellen Schreiber

Ellen Schreiber

Vampire Kisses 8

Cryptic Cravings

KATHERINE TEGEN BOOKS
An Imprint of HarperCollins *Publishers*

To my husband, Eddie, for being my high school crush

HarperTeen is an imprint of HarperCollins Publishers.
Katherine Tegen Books is an imprint of HarperCollins Publishers.

Vampire Kisses 8: Cryptic Cravings

www.harperteen.com
Library of Congress Cataloging-in-Publication Data is available.
ISBN 978-0-06-168945-1 (trade bdg.)

11 12 13 14 15 LP/RRDB 10 9 8 7 6 5 4 3 2 1
❖
First Edition

CONTENTS

"Rumors are spreading
that there are vampires living in Dullsville!"
—Becky Miller

Blood Exchange

I had to admit it, Dullsville was no longer dull.

In fact, for me, Raven Madison, the morbidly monotonous town I'd grown up in had finally become the most exciting place on earth.

Not only was I madly in love with my vampire boyfriend, Alexander Sterling, but I'd witnessed for the first time in my vampire-obsessed existence an actual vampire bite. The only problem was that it wasn't my neck being bitten.

This wouldn't have been such a tragedy for me if the recipient of the bite had been Onyx or Scarlet, the superfabulous Underworldy friends I'd met at the Coffin Club, but the bite was given to my own vampire adversary, a real vampire and gothic beauty, Luna Maxwell.

I'd been waiting almost a year to be bitten, since I'd met Alexander, not to mention my entire life of immortal dreaming, but for Luna it happened within hours of meeting another vampire. That night, on Alexander's lawn, there had been an amazing group of partygoers—a handful of vampires mixing with the mortal local students. It was something I'd never thought would happen. While playing spin the bloody bottle, Luna and Sebastian, Alexander's handsome and hapless best friend, had locked eyes and gone in for more than a juicy lip-lock. His fangs pierced the soft flesh of her swanlike neck. Luna had stared up at me, her eyes dreamy, as if she were some hippie tripping at Woodstock. She glowed even more radiantly than she normally did as a morbid fairy girl fashionista. Most of the partyers missed the action, but those who saw the bite passed it off as a macabre prank.

Sebastian had since moved out of the Mansion, and the rest of the vampires were perhaps back in Romania, or haunting the Coffin Club several towns away in Hipsterville. We hadn't gotten word of their whereabouts, and I hadn't seen any signs of them at Dullsville's cemetery.

For the week following the love bite, I tried my best to get Alexander's mind off his disappointment. He was suffering because his best friend's impulsive behavior had put not only himself and Luna but even Alexander's secret in possible jeopardy. Happily, tonight Alexander was finally obliging.

We were lying in the grass on a hilltop that overlooked Dullsville. From there we were able to see the glamorous sites of Hipsterville, such as the graveyard, but I didn't notice them because I was lost in Alexander's lips.

I hadn't broached the tender subject of receiving my own love bite with Alexander in a while. But I saw this evening, alone with him and without distractions, as my chance for another try.

Fiddling with a link chain hanging from his black leather belt, I asked, "Do you think it's easier for Sebastian to fall for a girl and to take her blood?"

Alexander furrowed his brow.

"Or was it easy to do what he did at the party," I continued, "because Luna is already a vampire?"

"I can't speak for someone else."

"But I want to know what you think."

Alexander paused. "Then yes, I think it's easier for him. He is very impulsive." His tone was clear and matter-of-fact.

I sighed.

Alexander reached for me and guided my hair back from my face with his fingers. "It means more to me than that," he said directly.

"Me too," I said, touching his shoulder. "But what if I were already a vampire?" I asked thoughtfully. "What if someone else turns me—not on sacred ground—so I won't be bonded to them forever. But—"

Alexander withdrew his arm. "That's what you want?" he asked, his voice almost cracking. "To be turned—by anyone? Sebastian? Or Jagger?"

"I was just thinking out loud," I quickly refuted. I didn't realize I'd hurt him.

"It would be that easy to have someone turn you? Just like that?"

When Alexander posed it to me like that, my fantastical solution didn't seem so romantic or practical in its reality.

"That's not what I meant."

"Are you so sure? You'd have my best friend bite you? Or worse, my longtime enemy?"

"But now you are friends with Jagger," I said, trying to lighten the mood.

"That's not the point."

"Of course not—I only want you. . . . I was just trying to take the pressure off of you. I was just thinking out loud."

Alexander didn't seem pleased with my response and continued to stare off into the distance.

"Let's be clear," I said, turning his face toward me. "I want to be a vampire. But I want to be one with you."

He barely broke a smile.

"I'm turning eighteen soon and you'll be seventeen," he finally said. "It's something I think about, Raven. You. Me. Our future. I want you to know that. But this is something that is life changing—especially for you."

"I know." I gazed up at my dreamy boyfriend's eyes. His face was so handsome in the moonlight. "But will you really be eighteen? Or something else, in vampire years?"

"I will really be eighteen," he said.

"And then the next year?"

"Uh . . . nineteen," he said as if I should have known.

"But you are immortal."

"The aging process will slow down. But that's many, many years from now. Is that what you are worried about? Us not being able to be together unless you are immortal, too?"

"I've always wanted to be a vampire, since I was born," I said to him urgently. "But then when I met you, I wanted to be one—to be turned by you. To have the covenant ceremony that you didn't have with Luna in Romania. A beautiful wrought-iron lace trellis with a coffin and two goblets, on sacred ground. I'd be dressed in a black corset dress and hold black roses. You'd be wearing a black suit and have a black rose in your jacket lapel. We'd say a few Romanian words and drink from each other's glasses. Then, you'd turn me."

"Wow!" he said with a laugh. "I guess you have thought about it, too."

"But it's not about me living forever. It's about me being romantically bonded with you and experiencing the world as a vampire." I stared up at him, the stars shining above him.

I waited for him to laugh, to think my ideas were childish and naive.

Instead he leaned into me and stared straight into my eyes, his chocolate ones dreamy and seductive. "There is a yearning that I have for you—that goes deeper than love," he said. "It's a desire that is palpable." He took my hand and raised it, exposing the inside of my wrist. "This desire courses through my veins," he said. He traced a prominent vein with his fingertip. "And yours. But I'd never put you before my own needs. What I struggle with isn't something that you should have to as well. It's a complicated life—more so than you realize."

"I know it's complicated. If you don't want to talk

about it . . ." I figured it was best to drop the subject. I didn't want to be a nagging girlfriend, and Alexander had been through so much already with Sebastian's antics. Why couldn't I be more patient and not spoil our pure quality time alone together?

"Well, you already know it's complicated," Alexander commented. "I'm not sure how I can keep convincing you."

I smiled. "I like it when you try," I teased. "But sometimes I worry that you'll leave the Mansion and return to Romania. And I'll be stuck here, alone for the rest of my life."

"Well, I am not planning on leaving."

"But you weren't planning on coming here, were you?"

"No . . ."

"See?"

"But I didn't have the same reasons to stay there as I do here," he said. "Is the only way I can convince you how much I care to . . ."

I waited. Maybe this was my chance to demand my need to be a vampire. But it had to be a decision he was ready for as much as I was.

"It isn't something we need to decide tonight, is it?" he asked.

If I said yes and his answer was that he wasn't going to turn me, what was I to do then? Normally I was daring. Adventure ran through my blood just as much as oxygen did. But this kind of risk—the emotional kind—was far different than sneaking into rumored haunted houses or cemeteries. This was my love life.

I gave him a puppy-dog face. "Of course not. But I wonder if it is something you want," I said with trepidation, "or is it only my fantasy?"

I waited. I knew Alexander had thought about it. We'd discussed it before. But as he said, he was going to be eighteen and me seventeen—and, most important, I was now being faced with watching other vampires bite. It wasn't something we could put off forever.

"I can guarantee you it's not just your fantasy," he reassured me. Then he glanced away, looking in the direction of the Mansion sitting atop Benson Hill. "You are so much like my grandmother . . ."

"But wasn't she lonely? For the rest of your family? Is that the fate you'd wish for me?"

Alexander faced me and stroked my cheek. "The only fate I'd wish for you is for us to be together."

My heart skipped a beat.

Slowly and seductively he leaned me back on the blanket. I gazed up at Alexander, the starlight filling my eyes. He began tickling me.

When I'd wrestled with Billy growing up, I'd learned to relax my muscles, which resulted in my no longer being ticklish. My little brother would run off, disgruntled, and I'd claim victory. But Alexander was no Billy Boy. I squirmed in my vampire boyfriend's powerful clutches and giggled like a little girl.

My head whipped side to side and my face hit something jagged on the ground.

"Ouch!" I cried.

Alexander released his grip. "Are you okay? I didn't mean to hurt you."

He helped me sit up. I felt only a slight bit of pain. But it was Alexander's reaction that disturbed me.

He was staring at my mouth.

"What's wrong?" I asked.

Alexander didn't speak. Instead his gazed was fixed.

I touched the corner of my lip.

A mixture of lavender lipstick and dark red liquid stained my ultrawhite fingertips. Oozing blood. To Alexander it was like an exotic perfume. Tantalizing and irresistible. Fresh blood to a hungry vampire.

I'd only been in this situation with Alexander once before, when he had come to my house to take me to the Snow Ball. I'd nicked my fingertip on the corsage pin. He'd had that same intense expression as he did now, only then I hadn't known he was a vampire, and I'd just quickly wiped the blood away.

But tonight was different. I knew that Alexander was a vampire. And the way he stared at me, so transfixed and intense, slightly frightened me but also made me feel wanted and alive.

Though this blood was my lifeline, Alexander needed my blood—or anyone else's—for his own existence. Others' blood was his lifeline.

Alexander wasn't repulsed by the sight and scent but intently attracted to it. I'd never witnessed it as much as I did today. It was apparent he was fighting his impulses. I wasn't sure if I wanted him to.

He shut his eyes and turned away from me.

"What would it be like?" I asked.

"Don't . . ." Alexander's appearance was scornful. Then his eyes softened. "I want to help you. Take care of your cut. But I can't. Don't you see how hard it is for me? I can't even help the one person I love. I can't come near you or I might—"

Alexander was fighting his natural impulse, and I was fighting mine. He rose up, his hands balled up in fists. He was biting his own lip. But I followed him.

I held my bloodstained fingers out to him.

I wanted Alexander to crave me more than he already did. Like Sebastian had craved Becky. But was that possible? Alexander was so intense and passionate as it was—was there anything deeper that he could feel or show me? And didn't he already crave me and my blood without me tempting him in this way?

I wondered if Alexander was right—that I might not like the vampire lifestyle after all, or that my lifelong dream of hiding from the sun and rising by the moonlight might not be as romantic as it seemed. Ultimately, becoming a vampire would be a decision I couldn't change. A test I couldn't retake. An ill-fitting dress I couldn't exchange. It would be for life. Forever. For eternity. But this wasn't about being turned. Alexander and I weren't on sacred ground. This was about something different.

My boyfriend stared at me, consumed by the scent of blood and the irresistible desire to devour it. "This is what you want? Me to be like the others—Jagger and Sebastian? Impulsive, needy?"

"No. I want you to be you. This was never about being anyone else," I said.

I could see Alexander was in turmoil. I was tempting him with something that was bigger than a fantasy to him. This was his everyday reality—a basic desire he had to fight against.

"It's okay," I said. I moved back and glanced away from him.

But instead of retreating, too, he stood still. I could feel his gaze fixed on me with a power that was hypnotic.

"No," he said. "Don't go."

I was surprised by Alexander's response and heeded his plea. I wasn't sure what he would do next. I almost gasped. Instead of leaving me, he stepped closer and took my face in his hands.

Alexander was so close to me, his alluring presence took my breath away. He slowly reached his hand to my cheek. I froze as if the events were happening in slow motion. As his firm hand slid seductively along my face, I melted with it. Then he tenderly wiped the blood from my mouth. It was as if he had touched my soul. My blood was now staining his fingers just as it had stained mine.

I waited with bated breath as the biggest moment of my life unfolded. I didn't think anything could have been dreamier than the first time we kissed or I slept in his coffin. Alexander was moments from taking my blood as his own.

I was suddenly filled with guilt and sadness as I thought maybe Alexander was doing this for the wrong reasons.

Maybe I'd just worn him down.

I took his hand and lifted my sleeve to wipe the dripping blood away. "You don't have to. . . ." I finally said.

Alexander gently blocked my hand with his free one. "I want to," he said intensely.

The moment seemed surreal, and I felt as if I were in a dream. My body flooded with warmth.

Alexander stared at the dewy blood droplets now trickling down the side of his ghost white palm. It was as if he was making the decision of a lifetime. This wasn't just any blood to him. It was *my* blood.

Alexander glanced at me and smiled. His sharp fangs caught the moonlight and glistened like icicles. Then Alexander drew his hand to his mouth. I watched, my mouth agape, as he took his bloody hand to his lips, pressed his hand to his mouth, and the red droplets disappeared. He inhaled a huge audible breath, as if he were breathing the life of me into him.

I gazed at Alexander. He appeared transformed. For a moment it seemed as if his pale complexion was almost alive. Alexander whipped toward me with unbridled intensity. He leaned into me, his hair flopping over his forehead, and kissed me with such force my knees shook and my flesh quivered. I thought I might die of heavenly bliss.

Alexander held me, limp in his arms, and I felt bonded to him in a deeper way than I'd ever experienced. He'd let me into his world, further than ever before.

Alexander squeezed me so tightly, it was as if we were one person. He picked me up and swung me around, the twinkling lights of Dullsville swirling by me.

When he let me down, we both were giddy and dizzy. When I regained my vision I could see my school, the country club, and the vacant Sinclair Mill off in the distance. It was then I noticed something unusual.

Alexander found me lost in thought.

"What is it?" he said. "I hope you aren't—"

"No—everything is fine," I reassured him. "It's nothing." I didn't want anything to break our perfect moment.

"What's wrong?" he insisted.

I had to squint to make out the object. It was then I could see clearly a familiar car—or, rather, hearse.

I tried to block Alexander's view by attempting to pull him away, but he didn't budge.

Alexander was already staring at the barren factory.

His blissful expression sharpened slightly, and I could tell it registered to him that it was Jagger's car.

I remained in his comforting clutches, bound to my love in a way I hadn't been before. We clung to each other, both reluctant to break our euphoric encounter and face the situation that we now overlooked.

So Jagger hadn't gone back to Romania or Hipsterville when Alexander's party was over. There had to be a reason why he didn't return and was apparently staying in the factory.

Alexander and I shared one last kiss before giving over to the distraction that lay at the bottom of the hill.

Not wanting to draw attention to us, Alexander parked the Mercedes in a grassy area more than fifty yards away from the mill. I was still beaming over Alexander taking my blood as his own. We tiptoed over the gravel road that led to the factory with a connection that couldn't be broken. As we neared the entrance, the dreamy look in Alexander's eyes continued and was only slightly marred by his concern over the discovery of Jagger's presence. We walked quietly through the shadows, and Alexander squeezed my hand extra tight.

The two antique smokestacks pointed toward the heavens like giant grave markers. The desolate and dilapidated factory was riddled with graffiti, broken and missing windows, rusted doors, and overgrown weeds and grass. Discarded boxes, trash, and beer cans were scattered around the grounds.

We turned a corner and came upon a vintage black mustang—Sebastian's ride.

Alexander stopped in his tracks. He sighed and slumped, let down by the discovery that his best friend was in the company of his former nemesis.

"Maybe Sebastian felt he had nowhere else to go," I offered encouragingly.

"Now that he's fallen for Luna," Alexander said, "he's probably under Jagger's spell, too."

Alexander took a deep breath and started for a white wooden door with the words "GET OUT" spray-painted in black.

"Well, then I guess we're going in," I said.

But instead of charging in, Alexander stopped.

"Maybe we should wait," he said, pausing at the doorway. "They obviously didn't want us to know that they're still here. Maybe we shouldn't let them know we found them."

"But how are we going to find out what's going on with them?"

"I could go in myself—undetected," he said, alluding to his nocturnal powers.

"That hardly seems fair," I said with the disappointment of a child who is told she is too short to go on an amusement park ride. "If I could change into a bat, I'd do it, too."

Alexander realized my limitations were upsetting me.

"Besides," I said, "it might be dangerous to leave me here alone in this dark, desolate place."

He nodded in agreement. "We'll see what we can find

out from here." Alexander cupped his pale and once blood-stained palm. I stuck my combat-booted foot in his cradled hands and he lifted me up. I struggled at first but managed to grab on to a ledge and pulled my head slightly above it so I could peer in through a broken windowpane. My black fingernails were in stark contrast with the gray cement.

Breathless, I peered in. At first it was hard to see. My vision had to adjust to the dim lighting. A flickering candelabra sat on a wooden table, and then I spotted a flash of white hair.

"Over there," I whispered to Alexander.

He adjusted his stance a few feet to our left to where I could now see clearly. Jagger was sitting with his back to me, his red-flamed Doc Martens boots resting up on a crate and his fingers woven together, supporting his white-haired head. He was the king of this crumbling castle. Sebastian, however, was fidgety. Alexander's best friend repeatedly pushed his dreadlocks away from his face, his many rings catching the candlelight. He didn't see me; perhaps the glare from the light above them hid me or he was so deep in thought he wasn't focused on anything else. He tapped his leg repeatedly, like a junkie waiting for a fix. I'd never seen him this frazzled.

"We'll need to start tomorrow," Jagger declared, "to get this thing up and running."

"So soon?" Sebastian asked.

"What are we waiting for?" Jagger countered.

Sebastian drummed his black-painted fingers on the table.

But Jagger and Alexander now had a truce, and Jagger wouldn't do anything to jeopardize that—or would he?

"The Coffin Club is a success," Jagger said. "So there's no reason not to start one here, too."

"This town isn't filled with vampires," Sebastian said. "Not like the other one, anyway."

"This town needs a place to dance," Jagger said. "For everyone to come alive—at night."

Sebastian couldn't argue with that. "I agree—there isn't anything to do in this town."

"And then the vampires will flock here. Like we did. Alexander, Luna and me, and now you. Mortals above and vampires below. The Coffin Club was a success and this one will be, too. We are sitting on a gold mine here in this abandoned factory."

"The Coffin Club Two?" Sebastian said.

"I already have a name for it: the Crypt."

"But are the preppy girls in this town going to want to hang out at a place called the Crypt?"

"I have ways to entice them besides the name alone," he said in a creepy but sexy tone.

"And vampires?" Sebastian asked skeptically.

"The mortals won't even know they're here. Besides, I have surprises planned for this club."

"What kinds of surprises?" Sebastian wondered.

"If I told you, then they wouldn't be surprises, would they? Besides, that's weeks away. We have a club to build first."

"What about Alexander?" Sebastian asked.

"He can be a partner, too. But I'm not sure if he's the type to own a club. He's very private."

"He is my best friend. I feel funny about this—without him being on board."

"*Is* your best friend, or *was*?" Jagger challenged. "Well, you'll have a place to stay here as long as you like."

Sebastian paused for a moment. He was the type that traveled constantly, his coffin covered with stickers from countries and cities around the world. It was something I could tell he was contemplating—a place to call home.

"But there is more of a vampire culture in bigger towns, am I right? Here it's just Alexander. And let's be clear. I think he likes it that way. I think we should respect that," Sebastian said.

Jagger cracked his knuckles, trying to mask his frustration.

"He escaped everything," Sebastian added. "Persecution from mortals and persecution from . . ."

"My family?" Jagger sat up. "The irony, you mean. That he'd travel so far away from my family and ultimately we'd wind up settling here, too?"

"You guys have a truce."

"I know. He helped my brother, Valentine. When Valentine was weakened and alone, Alexander cared for him and returned him to me. I'm not suggesting we restart that feud. But does that mean that what's good for Alexander is good for us, too?" Jagger asked pointedly. "Do we have to live our lives around his? Besides, maybe a vampire club is just the thing he needs. He won't be so alone on that hill with only a butler to attend to his needs."

"I'm just saying. I know he's still mad at me for what I did to Luna at his party. I know he thinks it jeopardized his existence here. And more of us coming to town—the kind that might be like me and act on impulse . . . it wouldn't be good for any of us."

"You were just being you. Just being us." Jagger leaned in. Even from far away, his blue and green eyes were piercing. "I can't help it if Alexander's more . . . restrained. He should have bitten Raven a long time ago. Why let it drag on?"

Just then my foot slipped and I knocked over the empty soda can on the windowpane.

"What was that?" I heard Jagger say.

"I think someone is outside."

I held my breath. Alexander did, too.

Alexander and I stood against the wall. A pigeon was walking along the window ledge.

Alexander tossed a twig near the bird. Startled, it flapped its wings wildly and flew off past the window.

"It's just a pigeon," I heard Sebastian say.

Alexander cupped his hands and helped me up again.

"You shouldn't be on edge," Jagger said. "Why are you so worried? It's just a club."

Sebastian thought, then finally spoke. "But it's a club with vampires—in a place that has been inhabited by only one. Alexander fights every day to be who he is and do the right thing. Just because you and I might be more alike? That doesn't mean he's the one that's wrong."

Jagger now was the one riffling his fingers through his white locks.

"I really want to run this past him," Sebastian said.

"And what's he going to say, yes? Besides, you can't tell him you've been hanging out here with me and Luna."

Sebastian hung his head low.

"Don't despair," Jagger said. "It's going to be awesome. Music blasting, drinks flowing, dancing until dawn. Beautiful girls everywhere. What's not to like?"

Sebastian's face lit up in the candlelight.

The Crypt sounded like the kind of club I'd want to hang out in. Just like the Coffin Club—but only a few miles from my house. I bit my lavender lip in excitement.

"I know he's mad at me . . ." Sebastian said, "but I still have his back."

"He'll see the club once it's open," Jagger said, rising. He put his arm around Sebastian. "It won't be too long. We'll decorate at night. I have ways of getting these things settled very quickly."

Sebastian bit his black nails.

"Just think it over," Jagger said, slapping Sebastian on the back like a coach does to a football player. "You have a place to stay, a new best friend, and . . ."

"A girlfriend," a sweet, ethereal voice said.

Just then pink hair bounced in from behind the shadows.

Luna was dressed in a wickedly cool frock—a pink mini-dress with black spiderwebbed tights. Her perfectly straight baby pink hair appeared as soft as something out of a shampoo commercial.

Sebastian shot up.

She took his hand and pulled him into her. They shared

a kiss that probably would have gone on forever if Jagger hadn't cleared his throat.

"It's Luna," I whispered to Alexander. "Now we should go in—"

Alexander helped me back to the ground and I told him what I'd heard. He shook his head. "We need to wait," he said.

"Really?" I was surprised by Alexander's sudden change in course.

"Yes," he said. "But not for too long. I'm always getting Sebastian out of predicaments. Maybe this time he needs to figure things out himself."

"But what about this new club?" I asked. "It will be here, in Dullsville."

"That we will have to fix. But I don't have to at this moment."

We heard the sound of a car driving over the gravel. Alexander pulled me back into an alcove.

A white Beetle painted to look like a skull drove past us and parked. Scarlet and Onyx hopped out of their car.

"I think it will be fun to hang with them here for a little while longer," Onyx said.

"That's because you want to be next to Jagger at all times."

"I do not!" she declared.

"It's okay," Scarlet reassured her. "I'd like to try to see that Trevor guy again.

He's such a prep—but I have to admit, I really think that's hot!"

Onyx giggled.

"Too bad I can't bring him here," Scarlet said. "Maybe I'll just show up at his school in his locker room."

The two girls giggled as Onyx opened the trunk.

"But he can't know about us," Onyx said. "That's why it's best to date vampires. We don't have to hide. Maybe you should like Sebastian?"

"He's all into Luna. That girl gets on my nerves. I sense something fake about her."

"Like she's not a real vampire?" Onyx asked as they retrieved several bags of groceries.

"No—like she's up to something. She's either really saccharine-sweet or totally aloof."

"Do you think she really likes Sebastian?" Onyx asked as they headed for the door with groceries in hand and passed by us.

"I think she likes—" Scarlet said, but we couldn't hear her answer. They had disappeared into the factory.

Alexander took my hand and led me away from the abandoned mill.

"I have other things on my mind tonight," he said, his eyes still dreamy from the blood exchange, and he drove me back to the Mansion.

As I lay in my bed, I cuddled Nightmare in my arms. Alexander had finally taken my blood as his own. The moment felt as intense for me as it was for him. To be one of the few living humans in the world to have blood taken by a vampire thrilled me beyond belief. And that it had been done in a harmless and loving way made the whole event exhilarating and blissful. The most important part to me was that Alexander showed me that he needed me, craved me, wanted me. The feeling of connection I now felt to him was stronger than blood.

And that moment was much different than when Sebastian had taken Becky's blood. One, she hadn't known it had happened; two, she wasn't aware that Sebastian was a vampire; and three—and most important—she wasn't in love with him.

With Alexander, this was something we shared together as a couple. He needed me—inside and out, just as I did him. Heart, soul, and blood. And if he'd done this, something I never thought he would do, did that mean that he was one step—a big step—closer toward turning me? I threw my head back on the pillow in laughter. At this moment, I didn't care about being a mere mortal. A vampire had taken my blood! I'd experienced much more beyond belief since meeting Alexander Sterling. I'd always dreamed that vampires existed, and now I knew. I'd fallen in love with one—and this very night, he'd acted as a true vampire and shown me how much he needed me.

But what should have been a uniquely blissful moment was complicated once again by the nefarious vampire twins, Jagger and Luna. If only I could spend time just thinking about Alexander. Finally our lives could be about just us. I wondered if that would ever happen.

I was torn about the Crypt. When I thought about what Jagger was proposing, a fabulous new dance club where none before existed, I was ecstatic. Practically speaking, though, there was nothing worse than having vampires (ones other than Alexander and his family, of course) inhabiting our town and mixing with mortals. If this place became a second Coffin Club, we could only guess what new vampires would do. Would they put the lives of unsuspecting students or townspeople in danger? But the other part—the dance club itself—was exactly what I'd really wanted all my life. A club, a haunted happening, only a few miles from my own house, that I'd be able to attend. A place, unlike school and all of Dullsville itself, where I would finally fit in.

My mind raced. Maybe I could help Jagger and the others with the plans, marketing, and decorating the Crypt. I could be the very thing they needed to bring life to the club.

Could this really be the gift I'd always dreamed of, and just in time for my birthday? But this one thing that would bring excitement into my life might bring disaster to Alexander's. The increase in vampires in Dullsville could bring attention to them and ultimately reveal the secret identity of the one vampire I cared about the most.

Or maybe, just maybe, this could be a place like the Mansion, where Alexander could finally be himself. No hiding or pretending to be anything but himself. Just drinking real Bloody Marys and dancing until dawn.

It was a gamble, knowing Alexander's former nemesis. Jagger was a vampire who craved attention and seemed to receive a lot because he owned a vampire club. Ultimately I was skeptical about his underlying intentions for this new club.

I was restless. For the first time in my life, the one thing I knew I needed to stop from happening was the one thing I wanted to make sure happened. Jagger, Sebastian, and the others were holed up inside the factory making plans for the Crypt while I was reduced to studying, homework, and insomnia.

W hat happened to your lip?" Becky asked when I hopped into her truck the following morning before school. "Did Alexander get carried away with you?"

"Is it that noticeable?" I pulled down the visor and checked my reflection in the mirror—an act I wouldn't be able to do if I were a vampire someday. I struggled with the idea that I would no longer be able to see myself and what that simple task would mean for me. To never be able to adjust things such as makeup, hair, and my clothes. Alexander was gorgeous naturally. I wasn't sure that I was ready for the world to see me without being able to present myself the way I wanted to be seen.

As I touched up my cut with corpse white cover-up, I felt a renewed sense of confidence. It wasn't the kind of confidence one feels when securing oneself with makeup but rather an internal assurance and peace. I felt as if I couldn't contain my glow.

"What's up with you?" Becky said. "You can't seem to stop smiling."

"I'm just in love. . . ." I said dreamily.

"Me too. We are both so lucky we found good guys. I still can't believe that we both have boyfriends, can you?"

"No," I said honestly.

We drove past the covered bridge that met the winding road leading up to the factory on the outskirts of town. I could see the smokestacks high above the trees, as if they were deliberately taunting me—reminding me of Jagger's presence.

"But I have so much on my mind," I said, slightly hinting to Becky.

"What's up?"

"If there was something you wanted to happen but it might be a threat to others, what would you do?"

"I wouldn't want it to happen."

"It's that simple?" I asked.

"Why would I want something that was not good for everyone?"

Becky was an altruist. That's why she was such a good friend to me. But in this case I would have preferred she be a bit more cynical.

"Why would it be bad?" she asked, worried. "Is this about you and Alexander?"

"It might not be bad," I confessed, and it was true, since I didn't ultimately know Jagger's plans. I was just going by his previous history.

"I think it would be easier if you just told me what you are talking about instead of being so cryptic."

"It's not really a threat, not now anyway," I said.

"I guess you'd have to take the threatening part away. That's the only way it would work."

I thought about what Becky said. If somehow I made sure that no vampires were invited to the Crypt, other than the ones already inhabiting the vacant mill, then maybe there wouldn't be a threat. I knew Onyx and Scarlet, and so far they didn't seem to take advantage of unsuspecting mortals. If Sebastian liked Luna, Onyx had her fangs set on Jagger, and we kept a close eye on Scarlet's fondness for Trevor, all the vampires would be accounted for. Perhaps it could be a fun place for Dullsville's high school students to hang out. They could, at last, finally understand what I've been craving all my life. Maybe the darkness could make them, too, feel more alive than ever. And it could be a huge, morbid playpen for me.

"You are a genius," I declared.

"Now are you going to tell me what you are talking about?"

Just then my cell beeped. It was a text from Alexander.

I can't sleep. Thinking of you.

I melted inside, knowing that my boyfriend was lying in his coffin and dreaming of me. And though I loved Alexander's mystery and old-fashioned style, I was grateful to be a not-so-normal girl with a not-so-normal boyfriend now that we were able to communicate like a normal couple.

I quickly texted back.

Miss you like crazy.

I held the phone out to Becky proudly. "Alexander," I said.

"I have something to tell you . . ." my best friend said as we pulled in to the entrance to school. "There are rumors about Alexander's party. Some people are saying Sebastian bit Luna. Like for real—like a vampire!"

"Why would they say that?" I asked skeptically.

"Someone swore they saw blood and the rumor snowballed. Now some kids are freaked out. They've been talking about it all week. I was kind of afraid to tell you. I didn't want you to be upset. But it isn't going away."

"So? That's all these people do is talk."

"But I think it doesn't really matter, since Sebastian and those guys aren't even here anymore."

They are still here, I wanted to say. I weighed my thoughts. I wasn't sure if it was time to tell her Sebastian and Jagger were sequestered in the factory, making a second Coffin Club.

"I kind of wish Sebastian hadn't left," she said in a tone that was mostly saved for a confessional. "Not because I like him—in that way—but there was something different about him. Like Alexander and that Jagger guy. I really can't put my finger on it. They're different from the guys here."

Because they are vampires, I wanted to say.

"It must be that European charisma," she finally said.

"Yes, that must be it." I smiled.

Becky pulled into the student parking lot and turned off the truck. "Your birthday is coming soon," she said excitedly as we got out and headed toward the main entrance. "What do you want to do? We could all go to Hatsy's or Hooligans."

"That wasn't what I really had in mind."

"The cemetery?" she asked nervously.

I smiled again. I hadn't thought much about celebrating my birthday. Ever since I was little, all my parties were duds and the only ones I ever enjoyed were when Becky and I just stayed up all night pigging out on brownies, chips, and super-sugared and hyper-caffeinated sodas and endlessly watching vampire movies.

"Alexander turns eighteen just before my birthday. I think we should just have one party together."

"That sounds awesome! Maybe we can have it at the Mansion," she suggested.

"Did I hear it's going to be someone's birthday?" a familiar male's voice said from behind me.

I didn't even bother turning around and continued walking, but that didn't stop my nemesis from disturbing me. He jumped in front of me, blocking my way.

"It's been a whole year, has it?" he asked in a syrupy tone. "Maybe this birthday I'll finally give you what you've always wanted."

Becky was shocked and blushed. But I wasn't moved.

Trevor was as menacing as he was gorgeous. If he were a vampire, he'd be the dark kind, the kind that sneaks up on innocent girls and bites without a thought. Trevor possessed many of the qualities of a vampire without actually being one. He constantly preyed upon me, was deeply charismatic, and tried to suck the life out of me.

Trevor could have any girl he wanted—except for me. But for some reason, I'd always been a thorn in his side, maybe one that he never really wanted to get rid of.

"I'll just have to Lysol myself and make sure to get a rabies shot," he said. "I won't turn on the lights. For my protection—not yours." He leaned in so close to me I thought for a moment he was going to kiss me.

"Don't forget to bring your 'Dating for Dummies' handbook," I said. "I'm sure you'll need it."

Instead of scowling, his face lit up with a glistening white, devilish smile. It was as if I'd made his day and our quick and battling banter were like an aphrodisiac to him. He winked at me before he arrogantly turned away and disappeared into the crowd of students.

Becky appeared weary as we headed to our lockers, but I remained unperturbed.

At the moment, celebrating our birthdays in a joint party should have been the biggest event in my life. Usually I'd be obsessed with thoughts of decorating the mansion with bat-shaped balloons, dark purple streamers, and a monster-size chocolate cake with tiny coffins.

But I couldn't think of anything else when Jagger and his friends were secluded in the vacant mill, designing its transformation into one of the most cryptic of all clubs. With Alexander's best friend only a short distance away from the Mansion, in secret, I knew I wouldn't be able to invite him or the others. It felt like a stake through my heart and made me miserably lonely for my boyfriend's sake.

The whole birthday celebration was already ripe with drama.

4

Creeping in the Crypt

I was dying to know more about the plans for the Crypt and Sebastian's sudden love for Luna. I had been hoping he'd be the perfect match for either Onyx or Scarlet, but he'd fallen for Alexander's former nemesis's sister. Now Sebastian would be hanging out with Luna and Jagger instead of Alexander and me and even going into business with Jagger. It was all happening too fast—even for someone as impulsive as me.

I decided I had a chance to find out more of Jagger's intentions that afternoon since I would be protected by the sun—I used it to my advantage.

As soon as Becky dropped me at my house after school, I hopped on my bike and pedaled toward the Sinclair Mill. The ride was exhausting, with its curving hills and narrow, winding roads.

The rocky gravel of the mill's driveway made it too

31

unwieldy to ride over even with my thick tires, and I didn't want to stir any sleeping vampires with the noise, so I walked my bike over the gravel and leaned it against one of the brick walls. I found a few rusted and locked gates with boarded-up windows.

I went around to the back of the building. This empty factory was historical to Dullsville, and I remembered learning about it in school. The mill prospered manufacturing uniforms for the war in the 1940s. After the war ended, a linen company bought it but it eventually went bankrupt. I imagined the noises of the running machinery cranking out uniforms for the war and the voices of the workers. The hours must have been long and laborious. I sweltered at school; I couldn't imagine what it must have been like to wear a floor-length heavy dress while sewing all day long. I thought it was hard to have worked at Armstrong Travel filing and making copies in a blouse, pencil skirt, and hose. I was happy I'd been born in the time of air-conditioning.

The red-tiled smokestack, once full of thick smoke, was now barely standing. What was once home to machines and laborers was now home to modern-day vampires.

I found the entrance that I had watched Onyx and Scarlet pass through. The door was unstable, looking like it might come off its hinges at any moment. I held it steady and gently opened it.

I quietly stepped over discarded materials and around garbage left by others' sneak-ins as I made my way to the main part of the factory. So far I didn't see any signs of the makeover I was hoping this empty mill would take on. Instead of neon signs adorning the walls and a tiled dance floor, spray-painted graffiti was the only decoration, and broken chairs were cast aside in the corners like litter. I knew the vampire crew wasn't in this room—the light was too bright for them to hide. They'd need a place dark and big enough to shelter five coffins.

As much as Jagger had been a pain to both Alexander and me, he did make the Coffin Club in Hipsterville a thriving place for both mortals and vampires to hang out. Jagger had a great imagination and was successful in seeing his vision come to life. And now I imagined how this factory could be transformed, too. I wish I'd thought of it first. But had it been my idea and my venture, the only thing that was sure was that no one would come. With Jagger, he already had vampires inhabiting it and hadn't done a thing to it.

The sunlight streamed in through cracked, broken, and vacant windows. This would be a hard place for a sleeping vampire to get any shut-eye. Last time we'd discovered Jagger's hideaway he was holed up in a freight elevator. But with so many vampires now in his company, that would be too small for all their coffins.

I found the two-flight staircase we'd once taken when Alexander and I had originally found Jagger here months ago. As I ventured down the rickety staircase, less light streamed in and I dug into my backpack and grabbed my flashlight. My free hand got tangled in several spider-webs.

"Sorry," I said to a grizzly-looking spider who stared back up at me.

I walked down a darkened hallway. It was straight out of a horror movie. There were no windows here in the sub-level hallway, and I only had a flashlight to show my way. My imagination transformed it into a mental institution, with screaming inmates. Not sure who or what might jump out at me, I had to fight my own will just to open a door.

I opened a few doors that led nowhere—empty rooms with no sign of life . . . or the undead. At the end of the hallway, I came to the last two doors—one across from the other. At this point I wasn't sure how much daylight I had to keep me safe. I decided to try the one on the right.

The door was secured, but not with a lock. It felt like something was wedged in front of it from the other side. To me that meant there was something behind it worth securing. I pushed against the door with all my might, and the wedge shifted just enough for me to slip through the opening. I stepped inside and cast my light around the room.

There they were—one right next to the other. Five coffins in a row. The first one, black with band stickers, was Jagger's. The second, baby pink, was no doubt Luna's. The third one was embellished with stickers from countries and cities across the globe, and I recognized it as Sebastian's. The fourth was black onyx stone outlined in white, and the fifth was adorned with shiny beads. Those were certainly Onyx and Scarlet's. Each had dirt around it in a circle. Five sleeping vampires, only a few feet away from me.

I imagined creating a custom coffin for Alexander and me—perhaps a double-wide coffin that looked like a huge heart. I wondered if the vampires were lonely in there, isolated from the rest of the world. I felt they must miss seeing each other during the daylight hours. Did they dream like we did or did they always have nightmares? I had to really contemplate this issue—think about if it was something I ultimately wanted, to be so closed away from another vampire or the outside world.

I knew I should back out immediately, return to the hallway, and close the door. I knew I shouldn't remain in the room or step any closer to the coffins, but I couldn't resist the temptation. I tiptoed up to Jagger's coffin. I paused briefly, then leaned my ear to the coffin lid. I heard the faint sounds of breathing.

Suddenly a thud came from the other side. I was so startled I jumped up and let out an audible gasp. My heart was racing so hard I was sure I'd have to call a doctor.

I paused, covering my mouth with my hand. I wondered if they had heard me.

Now I knew it was time to retreat. I tiptoed out and did my best to wrestle the wedge back underneath the door from the other side with my flashlight.

I checked the time on my cell phone and, with sunset approaching, realized I had only a few minutes to investigate further. I'd found the coffins and discovered that no plans had been carried out yet. But what was Jagger's next move, and were there any clues that could help me figure that out?

There was one more door left uninvestigated—the one across the hall from the sleeping vampires. I'd be smart to head to the Mansion and return another time with Alexander. I didn't have much time to decide, and I was desperate to know what lay on the other side.

I stared at the doorknob. I anxiously turned the handle, but it wouldn't open. I pushed and pulled so hard, the knob came off in my hand. As I wrangled it back on, I could feel it catching the latch. I did my best to be patient and opened the door slowly.

The room was dark except for a paper-thin beam of light streaming in through a broken window at least twenty feet from the floor. The smell of dust and mold filled the room. Old filing cabinets lined a few walls and there was an antique wooden desk. A green wine bottle with a Romanian label sat on it. In the corner was an aquarium containing not water but rocks and one very frightening tarantula. Gravestone etchings, including the very ones I'd seen at Jagger's place in Hipsterville, hung from the walls. This must be Jagger's new quarters. By appearances, he wasn't ready to return to Hipsterville in the near future.

I didn't have much time to riffle through the mess.

I spotted a tube of papers. I unscrolled them and discovered they were a stack of diagrams. Sticky notes labeled each one individually, the first, THE CRYPT, the second THE COVENANT, and the third, which was worn and appeared to be an original copy labeled SINCLAIR MILL. I was looking at the blueprints for Jagger's club.

I examined the one marked THE CRYPT. I wasn't in the

habit of reading blueprints and they weren't as detailed as I would have imagined. Instead of pictures there were boxes and lines, dotted and thick ones representing different things. I could make out one main room with a large box marked "stage."

So, was "the Covenant" the mysterious underground vampire club, like the Dungeon was in the Coffin Club? I knew Jagger had mentioned to Sebastian his dream to open the club to vampires. These could be the plans to prove that it was more than a dream.

I was intent on scouring it when I realized the light was no longer streaming in through the cracked window.

This meant one thing: The sun had set and the sleeping vampires in the next room were about to rise.

Alexander had to see these plans. He was smart and would know better how to read them. But I couldn't take them all with me. If Jagger discovered they were missing, who knows what he would do. I pulled out my cell phone to take a picture of them when I heard a rustling coming from the next room.

I would have to use my flash to take the picture, and I knew it would bring immediate attention to the room I was rifling through.

I only had seconds to decide. Ticktock. Ticktock. It was then I heard a creaking opening of coffin lid doors.

I decided against the photo. I definitely couldn't take all the plans, but maybe Jagger wouldn't notice if one was missing. I pulled away the one on top and rolled the others back up and bound them with the rubber band. My heart was pounding and the blueprints in my hands were shaking.

I rolled up the Crypt plans and stuck them in my backpack and replaced the other two exactly where they had been. I grabbed my flashlight and quietly closed the door behind me. I bolted out of the room and tore up the rickety spiral staircase before the vampires had a chance to reach the hallway.

Breathless, I hopped on my bike and pedaled straight for the Mansion.

"You did what?" Alexander exclaimed when I explained the last hours' events.

Alexander didn't greet me with the usual hug and sensual kiss. I realized I shouldn't have spoken so soon.

"I thought this way we could have leverage on their plans," I said. "Once you see this—maybe we'll know what he's really up to."

"Why didn't you wait for me?" he asked, shaking his head.

"It was the only way for me to find out info. Under the cloak of sunlight. Otherwise they'd be up and I couldn't have investigated. We need to know what they are truly planning."

I took out the blueprint and unrolled it on the antique dining-room table. I moved it far enough away from the several lit candelabras that wax wouldn't drip on the paper.

"I don't see anything unusual here," Alexander said, examining it like a professional. "It is the blueprint for the club. There's the stage, there's the bar. This is the dance floor. Over here is a door. Not sure where it goes."

"It seems really cool," I said, pining for the club that I wanted to have in Dullsville.

"But there was another set of blueprints," I confessed. "It said 'The Covenant,' but I couldn't get a photo of it in time. I think they are the plans for his secret vampire club. Would Jagger share everything with Sebastian?" I speculated, like Sherlock Holmes. "I don't think so."

"There was another set?" Alexander asked.

"Yes. I wanted to look it over—even take it—but I couldn't. The sun was setting and I didn't want to get caught."

"You shouldn't have taken these—you shouldn't have been in there in the first place."

"I know. But can we leave this to chance? Just wait until Jagger opens the club, when we both heard he plans to open it to vampires, too?"

"I wouldn't put it past him to do something. The Coffin Club was so successful, I can see why he'd want to open another one. But here? It's too dangerous."

"That's why we have to see those plans."

Alexander reluctantly agreed.

"I want to party at the Crypt so badly," I continued with a dreamy tone. "But we must stop this underground club and stop him from inviting more vampires to Dullsville."

"Raven, we must return these immediately, before Jagger realizes they are missing. He and I have a truce. I don't want anything to disrupt that."

I could see how important it was to Alexander to finally have the weight of the Maxwells off his back. I didn't mean to start trouble again. I was just trying to make sure that Jagger wasn't up to anything nefarious. But maybe I was misjudging Jagger's intentions, like people in Dullsville misjudged mine.

"And we have to examine the Covenant," I said to Alexander as I carefully stuffed the Crypt blueprints in my backpack, "just to be sure. I think it holds the real key to Jagger's plans."

Alexander shook his head again. He grabbed the keys to the Mercedes off the antique end table and we headed straight back to the factory.

Alexander and I parked the Mercedes at a distance and traipsed through the darkness toward the factory. I would have felt like a scolded child, with Alexander dragging me back to return my stolen goods, but Alexander knew, too, that we had to double check Jagger's intentions to make sure the club he was building was safe for Alexander's life in town and for the mortal residents of Dullsville.

We had three options. One, we could boldly go into the factory and face Jagger and Luna with my questions and admit I had their plans. Two, we could hang out and act natural, and while Alexander was chatting with the guys I could return the blueprint. Or three, both Alexander and I could sneak in and, with Alexander's nocturnal vampire vision, find our way to the office. The third was the riskiest, and thus, the most appealing to me. We both agreed that admitting that I'd taken the plans might be a cause for a broken truce, so we decided to attempt the full sneak-in.

It was a cool, windy night, and the leaves rustled in the trees as we passed by them. When we reached the gravel road we both sighed with relief. The road was empty of all familiar vehicles.

I showed Alexander the door I'd used to enter the factory and we quickly snuck in.

The empty, hollow factory rooms were just as I'd seen them a few hours earlier.

I illuminated the way with my flashlight, though Alexander could make out objects better than I could in the dark depths of the factory.

We descended the rickety staircase and I led the way down the narrow, dark, and dank hallway until we reached the last two opposing doors.

"It's this one," I said. I reached for the doorknob, but like the last time, it fell off in my hand.

Alexander's face grew serious. "Hurry!"

My hand shook as I stuck the knob back in its groove and tried to wind it so the latch would catch.

Alexander anxiously tapped his monster boots on the cement floor. The sound echoed, causing me to be more nervous than I already was. Finally, the knob caught the latch and we were inside Jagger's office.

I raced to the desk. The rolled-up blueprints were in the same position I'd left them. I quickly took off the rubber band and unrolled them.

"Here." I showed Alexander the second set.

Alexander peered at the plans. These drawings weren't as big as the Crypt's blueprints were.

"It looks like another club," I said, using what I'd learned by examining the Crypt's plans with Alexander.

"Yes . . ." he said. "Here's a small bar, a main stage, and a game room."

"The Covenant . . ." I said. "This room has to be the one Jagger's planning as the vampire club. It's underground and secluded, just like the Dungeon is at the Coffin Club. He said it himself— mortals above, vampires below."

Alexander shook his head, frustrated by what we'd just discovered.

"What's this?" I asked. I pointed to a small unmarked box drawn opposite the main stage.

Alexander and I froze when we heard noises coming from upstairs.

I could barely breathe.

"We've got to go," he said, replacing the Crypt blueprints on top of the ones for the Covenant. While Alexander headed for the doorway, I rolled them back up, being careful not to damage them in any way. I bound them with the rubber band and set them back into their original position.

Now that we'd accomplished the sneaking in part, we'd have to accomplish the harder part—sneaking out.

Alexander hung by the doorway as I grabbed my backpack and fumbled with my flashlight.

I could hear noises above us getting closer, and I did my best not to panic.

I tried to recover and tiptoed to the door, trying to avoid flashing the beam in Alexander's face. The light shook as I made my way between the desk and the filing cabinets. Suddenly my face banged hard into something.

"Are you okay?" Alexander whispered.

I felt the large metal object in front of me. It was cool to the touch and felt smooth. I'd walked into one of the filing cabinets.

"Are you okay?" Alexander asked again.

I was too embarrassed and shocked to feel any pain. I shined the beam on the floor as I continued toward the doorway.

"What's that?" Alexander whispered.

"What's what?" I wondered. "I didn't hear anything."

"That scent . . ."

"I'm sure it's just mold. This place hasn't been cleaned in years."

"It's not a bad smell . . . it's the scent of—"

It was then I felt the dewy drops on the side of my cheek. I must have broken open my wound when I ran into the cabinet.

I stepped into the moonlight. Alexander's eyes lit up, then he backed away.

Alexander didn't know what to do. If he got any closer to me, he might be attracted to my mouth, with lust and thirst. We didn't have time for a romantic vampire moment between us.

We heard the scuffling of footsteps coming down the staircase at the end of the hallway.

"They won't—" I said. "It's not enough and they are too far away."

Alexander put his finger to his lips to direct me to be silent as they came down the corridor.

"You must wipe it away. Before—"

My cut was small, but the scent of blood would be ripe on a breezy night in an empty factory. If the vampires were close, it wouldn't take long until they'd know a mortal was near.

"Do you smell that?" I heard someone say. I couldn't see them, but I could hear them shuffling around in their coffin room.

"It's blood," I heard a voice say. I couldn't tell if it was Sebastian or Jagger.

"It must be from the bottle in your office. You left it there last night," Onyx said.

"I finished it," Jagger said.

"It's human," I heard a female voice say. "Definitely not an animal."

"Yes, it's mortal. I could smell that a mile away."

"But why would anyone be here?" I recognized Sebastian's voice.

"It could be a homeless person," Jagger said. "I can't keep track of every nook and cranny of this vast place."

The voices were so close; I knew they had to be standing only a few feet away.

I pulled my sleeve over my fist and pressed it to the crease of my mouth.

Alexander's escape would be easy and painless and take

only seconds. In bat form, he could easily fly through the sky-high ceiling and out the crack in the window. I, on the other hand, had only two legs and a very impatient nature. Without someone to guide me out, I had only the help of my flashlight.

"I'm not leaving you here," Alexander said as if he was reading my thoughts.

"That handle gets stuck," I said. "Maybe that could ward them off for a few minutes. Push the door closed."

"There's no other way to escape," he said.

I could only hope they would let me be—but with such a temptation as my blood looming before them, now wasn't the time to find out. It was one thing for me to be in the company of Alexander. But it wasn't a good idea to be in the company of other, more impulsive vampires.

Alexander peered through the crack of the doorway. "They're in their room. Now is our only chance!"

He grabbed my hand and yanked me out of the room and toward the staircase. It was rickety and dangerous at best, but the elevator would be creaky and loud if it still worked. Not only would it draw attention to us—it could trap us in a cryptic cage.

We had just reached the stairs when the voices and footsteps emerged from the other end of the hallway. There was no time for a dash up and out. Alexander drew me behind the circular stairs and we stood close together in the shadows.

"Maybe I should tell Alexander I'm still here," Sebastian said. "What if he stumbles upon us, dude? He'd be, like, double mad knowing I hadn't told him I didn't leave."

"Why are we talking about this now?" Jagger said. "We might have an intruder."

"Because this is just as important."

"Why don't you wait until the club is up and running?" Jagger asked. "Then you can invite him. Wouldn't that be cool?"

"So, I just wait for months?" Sebastian said. "That's not cool, dude. Not cool at all. I have to face him again."

Just then Sebastian stepped away from Jagger. He was standing in plain view of me. I held my breath. My combat boot was sticking out clearly in his sight line. Sebastian eyed it for what seemed like forever. Our cover was blown. I was unsure what he was going to do next.

"That's it—" Sebastian declared. He turned his attention away from my boot and stared in Jagger's direction. "I'm going to the Mansion."

"Now?" Jagger asked. "But we have to find out who—"

"You said it yourself. It could be anyone. We can make a clean sweep of this place later tonight. But right now I have to talk to Alexander."

Sebastian started to go.

"Hey, hold on," Jagger said, grabbing his arm.

I continued to breathe as shallowly as possible.

"If you go—we'll all go," Jagger said. "I don't want you to be the only good guy in this situation."

"A trip to the Mansion?" I heard Scarlet say.

I heard more giggles and voices as they went up the steps and out of the factory, then car doors shutting and two engines starting. When we heard the cars drive out over gravel, Alexander and I tiptoed up the steps and peered out of a window to make sure they had really left and this wasn't a prank. The hearse was driving down the bumpy road, followed by Sebastian's Mustang. For a moment it stopped. Sebastian glanced back at the window where I was standing. He stared right up at me, sending horror-film-like shivers through my flesh. Then he turned away and drove off.

"Did you see that?" I said to Alexander. He nodded and put his arm around me, relieved. I tried to catch my breath, still nervous by our potentially dangerous vampire encounter. I began to soak in the gesture of Sebastian's good deed.

"Sebastian may be many things," I said. "But your best friend has still got your back."

Alexander and I went to the cemetery, where he cuddled me in his arms, trying to calm me down from our harrowing encounter, and we debated our next move. We sat together in front of his grandmother's monument, Alexander gently stroking my hair. It was still sinking in that he was so drawn to me in ways that most boyfriends aren't. He needed and craved me, thirsted for things about me that were only attractive to a vampire. Most girls at Dullsville High would be running away, but I was more attracted to him than ever.

Alexander had his arm around me but his thoughts were far away. I could sense the ache he felt for the strain on his and Sebastian's relationship. If Becky and I were fighting—which hardly ever happened—we'd apologize within minutes. But they were guys. I was happy that Sebastian had the strength to talk to Alexander. Alexander was relieved to know that Sebastian made the attempt.

And we figured this much: Jagger planned to open a dance club for mortals and vampires in Dullsville, and Sebastian was going to be his partner.

"Do you think Sebastian knows about the Covenant?"

Alexander shook his head. "He wouldn't be game for that."

"Even under their seducing powers?" I asked.

"Well, maybe . . ."

"What do we do now?" I asked.

"I guess we have to stop them from making a Coffin Club here in town."

"Do we really have to?" I asked.

"Are you kidding? Why the sudden change of heart? Weren't you the one trying to convince me that this could be dangerous?"

I sat up. "I love the Coffin Club."

"But it is full of underground vampires."

"What if this one wasn't? What if it was just full of the vampires we know?" I suggested. "Jagger could still have a club and you and Sebastian would have a place to drink your Romanian smoothies."

"The vampires we know? You saw how my best friend acted. How are they going to be partying with a bunch of mortals?"

I wasn't sure. I only knew I wanted the Crypt—a place I could dance in.

Closing the Crypt before it even opened meant I'd never even be able to experience the club at all. However, I didn't want the students of Dullsville to be in harm's way for my needs. There had to be a way to compromise.

"Maybe we can convince him to open the club just to mortals," I suggested.

Alexander thought. "I think it's a great idea. But I don't think he'll go for that. He wants the Crypt to be like the Coffin Club. To be the king of both worlds."

"Listen, Trevor's great at soccer. You are great at painting. And Jagger? He's great at making clubs. He can do it."

"Yes, I know. But does he want to?"

"He's so misguided. He wants to be loved like you and Trevor. He really does. He just doesn't see it because he was too busy trying to get revenge. But now that he's not? He could just be a success and popular owning and running this club for mortals."

"Again, I think that's a good idea—but you are talking about Jagger here."

"Alexander, I want this club. The Coffin Club is too far away for me to go to. My parents have the country club. Billy has Math Club. I don't have anything."

"What about me? The Mansion?"

"I love hanging out with you at the Mansion! Don't misunderstand me. But I'm pretty close to having my kind of club. A place for me to go to and have fun. I've never had a place like that anywhere."

"Well, you like Hatsy's Diner," he encouraged playfully.

"I do, if I want a burger. But I want to dance. I want to move and be in the darkness."

Alexander had traveled to cities and clubs around the world. Although he was a vampire, he'd been able to go to fun places that didn't see the light of day. I'd spent my life miserable in places where I didn't belong.

"But if we can convince Jagger to keep the vampires out and just let mortals in," I began, "then it can be a club like any other. And there isn't a club anywhere near here for teens to party. I'm sure he'd get a crowd. It would be a win-win situation for him."

Alexander wasn't convinced.

"We'll have to persuade him that it's in his best interest to keep the club," I pressed.

"Are you going to tell him?" he asked with a coy grin.

"He's not going to listen to me," I said. "But he'll listen to you. He'd have to."

"Would he?" Alexander wondered. "Jagger and I have a truce. But further than that? I'm not sure that I could convince him to open his club any way but the way he wants to."

I sighed. "But I fantasize about the Coffin Club. It was awesome—the music of the Skeletons blasting against the walls. Those freaky mannequins hanging from the ceiling. The coffin lid doors. And the secret dungeon."

"And Phoenix . . ." Alexander laughed.

"Yes, Phoenix," I said, recalling Alexander's purple-haired alter ego who convinced Jagger to keep the Dungeon a secret. "I was crazy about him as well. Not like you, I mean. But *like* you."

Then it hit me.

"What if he came back?" I wondered aloud. "What if Phoenix made sure that the club remained only mortal? Except for you, Sebastian, and the others, of course. But the Covenant would remain closed."

Alexander thought for a moment.

I was sure this was a great idea. "Phoenix was able to keep peace when Jagger was trying to make the Coffin Club nefarious and bring in more vampires," I said. "Phoenix stood up against Jagger, with the club members by his side, and forced him to keep the clubsters happy by keeping it a secret and civil club. He can do the same here by keeping it mortal."

"I'm not so sure . . ."

"And if Jagger doesn't want to listen, Phoenix could threaten to go back to the Coffin Club. He could shut down that club—Jagger's flagship location. Jagger wouldn't let anything jeopardize the Coffin Club again. Phoenix is ultimately the only one with real power over Jagger."

Alexander fiddled with a dandelion in the grass.

"I'd love to see him again," I said, taking another approach. "That sexy purple hair. That hot rod motorcycle. Those tight black pants. And now that I know it's you," I said, sidling up to Alexander, "I might even be able to give him that kiss he was looking for."

"Hey, don't be cheating on me with me," he teased.

"Oh, it would be so cool. The Crypt. Dancing together

and hanging out with Scarlet and Onyx. Dullsville has come alive since I met you."

I rested my head on his shoulder as I fantasized about the Crypt; Alexander was lost in thought, too. I'd put a lot of ideas in his head. I decided to change the subject.

"Our birthdays are just around the corner," I said. "Becky wants to know what we're going to do."

"We should celebrate them together," he offered.

"That's what I said!"

"We could throw a joint party," he suggested.

"Really? That would be the best birthday ever!"

"And I think I know just the place," Alexander said. "It's called the Crypt."

6

Club Rumors

The following day, Becky caught up to me after Language Arts class.

She ran up and grabbed my arm, bursting to tell me major news. "I heard that Dullsville is getting a new club!" she said.

I was shocked. Gossip traveled so fast in Dullsville it was scary. But this breaking news had found its way to Becky particularly fast. I had to wonder if Jagger was spreading it himself.

"What did you hear?" I asked.

"Just that there's going to be a club—for us!"

"A club? Here?" I acted surprised, but really I was. Not that there was going to be a club—but that the word was out about it already.

"Yes. And you don't have to be twenty-one to get in. It's going to be awesome!"

"Did you hear where it's going to be?"

"No, but as soon as I find out, I'll let you know."

The irony was that Becky was telling me about the club I should have been telling her about all along. She was going to scavenge for information that I already knew. I felt guilty not telling her, but until I knew for sure about Jagger's true intentions, I didn't want to add gossip to the mill.

"I can't wait," Becky said. "It will be fun to have a place to hang out and dance with Matt."

I froze. My innocent best friend was planning on coming to the club—the one that Jagger would be inviting unknown vampires to?

"You can't go—" I blurted out. "I mean, I don't think it will be your type of club."

"Why not? It's open to everyone."

That's the problem, I thought. Mortals and vampires, too.

Would I have to protect Becky from the modern vampire world forever? It appeared I would, at least for the near future.

"I'm just saying," I began, "if the popular crowd is hanging out there, then it's not going to be a fun place for us."

"It's supposed to be awesome. Matt and his friends will be going. I'm sure it will be fine—we can hang with just us. We'll just keep to ourselves. And besides, clubs are dark and loud. I've seen them on TV."

"Did you hear that there's going to be a place to rave?" a Prada-bee a few lockers away said to her friend.

"I've heard about it," the friend said. "But I don't have any info."

"It would be so cool. We don't have anywhere we can dance. At least not without a fake ID." The Prada-bee laughed a snorty laugh.

"Where is it going to be?" her friend asked.

"I heard it's going to be in that abandoned church." The Prada-bee spoke in a whisper.

"I was told they're renting out the country club on Friday nights," her friend gushed.

"Who is 'they'?" the Prada-bee asked.

I leaned in.

"I heard they're going to have it in the graveyard. Surely you'd show up," Trevor said, spotting me eavesdropping. "Last to know, as usual?" he asked.

I didn't even bother with a response.

"Perhaps another highly anticipated event you won't be invited to?"

"What? You have to be invited?" I asked, breaking my short silence.

"For the opening, of course," my nemesis said. "They aren't going to let just anyone in."

"They are my friends, not yours," I said. "Believe me, I can make sure you don't get past the bouncer." I shut my locker.

"Don't be so sure," he said. "I'm on the VIP list." He slithered up to me so close I could smell the peppermint gum he was chewing. "And if there is a new hot spot club, you'll be needing a date," he said coyly. He took my hand

and before I could withdraw it, he wrote his number on my palm.

Becky passed me hand sanitizer and I did my best to rub it off.

So the Crypt's grand opening was by invitation only? Jagger was killer on getting the buzz started. He hadn't even started to decorate. By the time he did open, he'd have the whole high school lined up around the block waiting to get in.

And I wasn't sure that was such a great thing after all. The students here would be exposed to unknown vampires. Once the drinks were flowing and the heat of the dance floor kicked up, who knew which of these mortals would be hanging out with, kissing on, or being driven home by vampires from other towns? And though most of the students had contempt for me and had made my life here in Dullsville hell by either ignoring or teasing me, I couldn't let their materialistic lives be in danger. And if anyone in this town was going to fall prey to a handsome vampire, it was going to be me.

Becky and I were hanging out on the soccer field's bleachers shortly after the sun set. I was doodling in my journal, drawing pictures of what I wanted the club to be like and ideas for gifts for Alexander's upcoming birthday. I was set to meet him in an hour, after he'd awoken and had dinner. I was killing time by doodling as the soccer snobs competitively kicked the black-and-white ball up and down the field against the opposing Tigers.

"Remember when we were here at the game with Sebastian?" Becky asked, referring to when Alexander's best friend first arrived in Dullsville.

"Uh-huh . . ."

"I took a picture. Of you and him."

"Yes . . . I remember," I said. Then it hit me what Becky had just told me.

"Well, the weirdest thing happened. I was flipping through the photos on my phone and he's not there."

"You must not have saved the picture," I said. "I do that all the time."

"No—that's not what I mean. He isn't in the picture."

That was what I was afraid of. "You probably moved it," I told her.

She picked up the phone and showed me. "Look."

I saw a picture of me, smiling and angled, as if I was leaning my body against someone. Only there wasn't anyone else in the picture.

"Isn't that odd?" she said, perplexed.

"Well . . . maybe he shifted out of view."

"I don't remember him doing that."

"Or maybe you moved the camera. That happens to me all the time."

"I know. But the way you are sitting—if he had moved, you would have fallen over. And there is still this space. And if I moved—then there wouldn't be all this blank space where he'd been. I can't figure it out."

"Looks like they are going to score . . ." I said, attempting to change the subject.

"Don't you admit it's weird?" she stressed.

What was I going to say? *You took a picture of a vampire. What do you expect?*

I shrugged my shoulders.

"I thought you of all people would freak out. It's almost like out of a scary movie."

Becky shoved the picture in front of me again.

"Yes. It is weird. But I'm sure he just moved away at the last minute. That's all."

I returned to doodling in my journal.

"I guess," Becky said. "But I'm saving this picture. I was hoping to have a picture of Sebastian. At least I have a cool one of you."

The game was over and I saw Trevor hanging out by the trees. He was resting his arm against a trunk and was posing in a seductive way that led me to believe whomever he was talking to was of the female persuasion, and of the pretty kind. It was unlike Trevor to be secretive with his women, so I became curious. As he continued to talk and pose, the girl remained hidden in the shadows. After a few minutes I noticed something illuminated by the field lights—bright scarlet hair—the kind that came from a bottle, not used on any of the girls at our high school.

"Where are you going?" Becky asked as I leaped over the bleachers and raced down the metal stairs.

So that's who's leaking the info. Jagger must have put her up to it, I immediately surmised. If Trevor's on board, then Jagger is sure to have a crowd. Jagger knows Trevor will tell the whole school, along with the whole town.

"Oh, Scarlet!" I said.

She looked surprised to see me, and stepped even further back into the shadows. Trevor also seemed taken aback by my presence.

Just then Matt called to him as the team headed toward the gym. Trevor paused. It was odd for him to have two goth girls in his company. He was used to being surrounded by preppy, conservative types. He was reveling in his rebellious attraction to us.

"I've got to go. . . ." Trevor said reluctantly. I knew he wanted to stay with us, but it would have to remain a fantasy for him.

The way he lingered in front of us by the tree, it was as if he wanted to kiss one or both of us, but he wasn't brave enough to make a move on Scarlet in front of me. And he knew if he kissed me, I would slug him.

"Is that Trevor's number?" she asked, noticing the smudged digits on my palm.

"Yes, and I tried to burn them off. I told you—he's not what you think he is." I paused for a moment.

When we were alone, I said to her, "After Alexander's party, you all just left."

"Yes. I'm so sorry it ended so quickly."

"So, are you in town long? Will the others be joining you?" I asked with pretend innocence.

"I can't lie to you, Raven. We're all still here."

I was so relieved my friend was confiding in me about what I already knew. I would have hated for her to have turned out to be a false friend. She had accepted me as a vampire, and then when she found out my true identity, she accepted me for being a mortal. She was a better friend to me than I'd been to her. And because she and Onyx didn't have the history with Alexander or the cunning actions and animosity of Luna, they were the type of vampire girl friends I'd longed for all my life.

"I was so sad when you guys left," I said. "I knew you had to, but I was really bummed. I am relieved knowing you're still here."

"I wish we could hang out," she said sincerely. "But don't tell Jagger you saw me if you run into him. Please."

"I won't," I said. I hated that he had a hold on her. He was providing her and her best friend with room and board, and I'm sure she didn't want to jeopardize that. But I wanted to hang out with them and didn't want him to get in the way of my fun. "Why don't you and Onyx meet me tonight at the cemetery?"

"Yes, that's a great idea! We can have some girl time!" she said, giving me a hug.

Then Scarlet disappeared into the night.

7

Ghouls Night

I called Alexander and explained I'd be a little late for our date since I wanted to meet Onyx and Scarlet at the cemetery. He agreed it was a good idea to get information from the girls and invited me to the Mansion when I was finished. Though I was excited to spend some time with Onyx and Scarlet, I pined for any missed hours not spent with Alexander, since we were separated for all of the daylight hours.

When I arrived at Dullsville's cemetery I found the grimmest sight; deep within the graveyard I spotted two goth girls sitting on tombstones, their legs dangling over the headstones—one wore white-and-black striped tights, the other torn black tights.

When they noticed me they both rushed in my direction.

"It's so great to see you, Raven," Onyx said.

"Jagger told us not to tell you we were here—" Scarlet blurted out. "For Sebastian's sake, he said. We shouldn't have listened." Scarlet was remorseful.

"But he's giving us a place to stay—" Onyx said defensively.

"And Onyx has a major thing for him," Scarlet blurted out.

"I do not!" Onyx retorted.

"Don't lie." Scarlet was brazen.

"So what's the real deal?" I asked.

"Jagger plans to open a club called the Crypt," Scarlet said as if she was sharing breaking news.

"Will it be like the Coffin Club? With a secret dungeon?" I asked.

Onyx nodded.

"He's hoping to invite vampires from around the area," Scarlet shared.

"There aren't vampires around this area," I said. "It's only Alexander."

"Well, Jagger wants the Crypt to eventually be as big as the Coffin Club," Scarlet said.

"But it's just not a good idea," I urged. "Not in this small town. Everyone knows everything and they all gossip. It will be harder to conceal yourselves," I warned.

"We are good at being secretive," Scarlet reassured me. "It's our life."

"I know," I said. "It's one thing to go underground in a bigger city. But here? People will find out easily—then you'll all be in danger," I told them.

"I don't know," Scarlet said. "We are always in danger. It's part of being a vampire in a mortal world."

"But here you could be one of the few—the special ones." I tried to convince her.

"But it's hard to meet other vampires," Scarlet said. "The Coffin Club is special for us. It's a place to be ourselves and not have to hide. Do you know how hard it is to hide every waking minute of every waking night?"

I didn't answer as she stared at my outfit.

"Of course you don't," she said. "You are bold and outspoken. Everyone in this town knows you are different. You are yourself. I don't think you realize how hard it would be for you to be a vampire. That there would only be a few mortals you could know. That you couldn't be your whole self in public, like you are now."

It was one of the parts of being a vampire that I thought would be the hardest for me. I'd spent my life being truthful about who I was, what thoughts I had, my style and tastes. Finally getting the bite of my lifetime would change all that in an instant. But at this moment, we weren't really talking about me being a vampire, and I needed to fight to make this club Jagger was opening a safe one for Dullsville.

"I totally understand and get your position," I said. "But in this town, the Crypt wouldn't be like the Coffin Club. In Hipsterville, everyone is accepted for being a hippie, a goth, or whatever. They're even embraced for being different, and no one digs any deeper. Dullsvillians fear the kind of people they don't find in their country club on the back nine, tennis courts, or cigar bar. I really can't stress enough that the vampire part of the club here would not be like the Dungeon. It can put your existence in jeopardy.

You have to believe me—you know I'm in love with a vampire. His needs come before my own. I want what's best for him and all of you."

Scarlet softened and gave me a hug. "We really were lucky when you arrived at the Coffin Club. If only all mortals were like you, we wouldn't have to hide at all and our world would be much better."

"Maybe we should say something to Jagger?" Onyx asked shyly.

"That would be awesome," I chimed in. "But he doesn't have to stop the entire club—just the vampire part."

It was then I realized that what I said might be hurtful.

"But what would be the point?" Scarlet asked, offended. "Mortals have their clubs everywhere."

"I'm sorry—I didn't mean that about you. I meant nefarious vampires," I said in an apologetic tone.

"I know . . ." she said.

"But truthfully," I went on, "we don't have a club here. The Crypt could be that club, and you could be there, too. But other vampires? That's the part that won't work."

Onyx and Scarlet thought for a moment.

"Well, I can't tell him what to do," Scarlet admitted. "But maybe Onyx can."

"Me?" She made a sheepish face. It was evident she adored Jagger far too much to be able to stand up to him.

"What about Trevor?" Scarlet asked.

"He can't know about any of this. Not vampires. Not Alexander. Not you," I said. "We must make a pact," I said, "that we all will do our best to persuade Jagger to open the Crypt to mortals only—and VIVs—Very Important Vampires. You guys, Sebastian, Luna, and of course, Alexander."

We all put our pale hands out, one on top of the other, our wicked nail polish disappearing in the darkness. "We promise," we said in unison. Then we released our hands.

"And maybe, someday—you'll come in as a mortal and leave as a vampire?" Scarlet teased.

"That would be awesome!" I beamed. I had a few more minutes before I was to meet Alexander, so I could talk with the girls before I headed to the Mansion.

"So what's it like living at the factory?" I asked them.

"It's fun," Scarlet said. "We miss the Coffin Club because there were more vampires to hang out with. But we were hoping that this one . . ." She paused. "But now that you told us," she continued, "I see your point."

"And Scarlet likes being close to Trevor," Onyx blurted out.

"Does he know that you're a vampire?" I asked.

"No!" she said. "I don't kiss and tell."

Scarlet kissing Trevor. The thought was too much for my stomach to take. I knew that Trevor was going to be unfaithful to my friend. I didn't want her to be used like so many of his girls.

"He's not all that you think he is," I said.

"Hot? Gorgeous? Athletic? Rich?" Her face lit up like she was surrounded by candlelight.

"He's trouble," I said.

"I'm all about trouble." Scarlet laughed.

"We wish you were a vampire like us so you could hang out at the Crypt full time," Onyx said.

"I do, too," I agreed dreamily. "And what's the scoop on Sebastian and Luna?" I asked. "Does he really like her?"

They nodded in unison.

"And does she really like him?" I asked.

"She acts like she does," Scarlet began. "Always fawning over him and flashing her pink eyelashes. She gets on my nerves." Then she looked at Onyx. "But she could be your future sister-in-law, Onyx Maxwell!" Scarlet teased.

Onyx blushed.

"Well, I always felt something odd about her," Scarlet said seriously. "Like I can't trust her."

"Me too," I said.

Scarlet and I had a common bond. She was feisty and strong and didn't let the average person—or vampire—get in her way. If she wanted something, she went for it, and any obstacles in her way were just a minor inconvenience. And I knew she was honest and good-hearted. I was just unhappy that her romantic affections were for Trevor. If her heart was set on it, convincing her not to go after Trevor would be like convincing Jagger not to open the Crypt.

"We gotta run," Onyx said. "We have to get back to Jagger."

"So when are you coming to the Crypt?" Scarlet asked.

"It's not open yet," I said.

"I know, but we're starting to decorate tomorrow night."

"Then I'll be there!" I said with a wicked grin.

* * *

When I arrived at the Mansion, I found a familiar car parked in the driveway and an even more familiar guy sitting on the steps.

"Alexander won't let you in?" I asked Sebastian.

"I haven't had the courage to knock yet. I'm not sure what I'm going to say."

"All you have to do is say something."

"I tried—last night," he said. "But you already knew that." He shot me a look that reminded me of the moment he caught us sneaking around the mill.

"What you did last night—that made a huge difference," I said. "Alexander knows you have his back."

"What did you hear?" Sebastian asked.

"That there is going to be a new club," I said.

"Yes . . ."

"It's going to be in the factory," I added.

"Uh-huh," he acknowledged.

"And that it's open to mortals and vampires," I told him.

"Oh." Sebastian bit his black fingernail.

"Are you seriously game for that?" I asked.

"Well, since I'm a vampire, I guess that's fine for me." His dreadlocks shook as he laughed.

"You know what I mean."

Sebastian sighed. "Of course, I don't think it's a great idea for this particular town. But Jagger is so convincing and Luna is hypnotic. I'll do anything she asks."

"Do you know anything specific about the underground club? What it's called?" I hinted, wanting to see if Sebastian had any goods on the plans for the Covenant.

"No," he said. "I just know he wants to make this club like the Coffin Club."

"You know that it's a really bad idea to open it to outside vampires."

"I can see it would be a problem."

"And you need to know, Alexander is against it."

"He is?"

"Yes! He has lived in peace in this town since he arrived. And it isn't just about him. He'd never sacrifice the good of all for what's good for him. That's not in his nature. But he loves my family and his new friends here. He doesn't want to put them in harm's way."

"And you?"

"I agree. It could be a catastrophe. If the Dullsvillians run you all out of town, you don't lose anything. But me and Alexander? We lose everything. And what if a vampire comes here and does what you did to Luna to some unsuspecting mortal girl? And what if everyone sees it? How do you think this town would respond?"

"It is really complicated, isn't it?" he asked.

"No, it's quite simple. The Crypt should be a mortals-only club. Then everyone could be safe—and you and Onyx and Scarlet could live here, too. Really close to your best friend."

"That would be cool," he said with a smile.

"Jagger wants money and he wants power. He isn't seeing what is already here. A small town with a close-knit, albeit boring, community. But for you, Alexander, and the girls, it's a great haven."

"Yes, otherwise we could make this town be like any other."

I was happy that Sebastian seemed to be on the same page as Alexander and me. Because of Sebastian's laid-back nature, I had figured he might be swayed by the crowd he hung around with at a given moment. Although I had a feeling he would ultimately be in favor of a safe and mortal club, just like his best friend.

"What were you going to say to Alexander when you came to the Mansion last night?" I asked.

"That I messed up again. Last time I crossed the line with Becky, and now, I made him mad by biting Luna. But I just couldn't help myself. I was caught up in the moment. I'm not the kind of vampire Alexander is."

But some things weren't so different between them now. I could have told him that Alexander had taken my blood, shared his coffin with me. That the vampire things Alexander and I shared were very meaningful. But it wasn't my business to tell our secrets to Alexander's best friend.

"And I want to convince him that my feelings for Luna are different," Sebastian added.

Oh boy, I thought. That was not what I wanted to hear.

"A girl wants to be special," Sebastian said. "I tend to like a lot of girls. First Becky. Now Luna. If we'd been dating, you would have become a vampire a long time ago."

The idea penetrated me. If I'd been with a different vampire, I might already be one by now.

But that wasn't what I wanted—to be turned by a

vampire's desire alone. I wanted it to be special, permanent, and romantic. And I wasn't the kind of girl to settle, either. Especially since I'd fallen in love with Alexander.

"Alexander's looking for the right girl. Other vampires would bite a girl and never see her again."

That did sound horrible. To be changed and then abandoned. "Have you done that?" I asked.

"No, but I've been close."

I hung on his words.

"Alexander changed his life for you," he said. "He didn't return to Romania when he could have. He fought to buy his house so he could continue living here to be close to you."

Hearing Sebastian say how much Alexander cared meant the world to me. I'd always wanted to do the changing, but Alexander had changed for me.

"I just know with Luna, this time it's for real," he said.

"How can you be so sure?"

"She's amazing. She's beautiful and sexy. I can't take my eyes off of her."

I didn't care to hear how wonderful Luna Maxwell was. "Would you change your life for her?" I challenged. "Never travel to all those cities without her?"

Sebastian thought. "Yes. I think I would."

"Then I think you love her," I said through gritted teeth.

Although I wasn't crazy about Alexander's best friend falling for the one vampire I couldn't trust, it was better than him turning his affections toward Becky again. I would have preferred for him to fall for Scarlet or Onyx, but no amount of my morbid matchmaking seemed to make that happen.

My cell phone beeped and I noticed I had a text from Alexander.

Where are you? What's taking you so long?

I texted back, Meet me at your front door.

The front door slowly creaked open.

Alexander looked surprised to see Sebastian standing next to me.

"Dude—" Sebastian said. "It's time I finally . . ." he began.

He waited for Alexander to say something—anything—but my boyfriend remained silent.

"How about another game of Medieval Knights?" Sebastian said. "You can get even with me in the virtual world. The best two out of three wins."

A huge smile came over Alexander's face. He pulled the front door wide open and Sebastian sauntered inside. I gladly followed the two upstairs to the Mansion's TV room.

That was it—no groveling or tearful reunions. No hugs or major blowouts. Just a face-to-face, over-in-a-minute reconciliation between two childhood best friends.

I sketched my ideas for the Crypt while two vampires battled out their angst against each other with computer-generated swords.

There were a few things I felt good at: sneaking into mansions, getting in the face of brazen bullies, and decorating in the style of the macabre.

I wanted to share my ideas with Jagger because I was sure that I could help out with the opening of the club. I could design, decorate, or even clean. I didn't care. I'd sweep floors if I had to. When I worked at Armstrong Travel, there wasn't anything I wanted to do—and I was being paid. However, for a chance to be part of the Crypt, I'd be willing to do anything—well, almost anything—for free.

The next night, before I headed to the Mansion to spend time with Alexander, I raced to the factory to plead my case for joining the Crypt's crew.

I found Jagger in one of the main factory rooms pacing and talking on the phone. When he caught sight of me, he quickly ended his call.

"I guess Sebastian told you we were here?" he asked.

"I figured it out on my own," I said triumphantly. "I want to talk to you about something."

"Yes?" Jagger seemed pleased. He dusted off an old chair and offered it to me. "Please sit down."

I obliged and took a seat.

"What can I do for you?" he asked intently. If Jagger wasn't so nefarious and creepy and Alexander's onetime enemy, he would actually have been sexy. His white hair was jagged and edgy, and his mismatched eyes were intense and mesmerizing. And there was something attractive about the word "Possess" that was emblazoned across his upper arm.

"I'd like to help you with your club."

"Really . . . ," he said in a tone that revealed he was clearly as surprised as he was suspicious.

"I'm great at decorating. I can help find fun things around town."

I realized I might be treading on his ego. After all, he did run the Coffin Club. Who was I to tell him he needed help to design a successful club?

"Of course, I know you are really good at it, too," I continued.

Jagger sized me up. "I could use an extra hand," he finally said. "But what about your boyfriend?"

"I'm not sure he'll want to help."

"Yes, I guessed that. But will he mind us working so closely together?" Jagger whisked back his white locks confidently. "What if you wind up preferring my company?" He grinned, his fangs catching the light of the flickering candelabra and his blue and green eyes piercing through me.

But I wasn't interested in his romantic inferences. "I don't think that will happen, and he's not the jealous type."

"I imagine he knows about the Crypt?"

"Uh . . . yes."

"And what does he think of the idea? He didn't seem keen on it when I brought it up to him and Sebastian at his party."

"I don't think he likes it any more now than he did then."

"But you do?"

"I love the Coffin Club," I gushed. "And I want a place where I can hang out here in Dullsville."

Jagger beamed. His pale skin radiated with the glow of my compliments. He rose, taking in his surrounding as if he was imagining the new club.

"But there's that whole thing about . . . vampires," I said.

"That bothers you?" He leaned over me, his hair hanging sexily over his eyes.

"Yes." I did my best to confront him. "I think this club should be for mortals only."

"I thought that a vampire club would be up your alley."

I stood up. "Uh . . . it is," I said sincerely.

"You want to be one," he said, stepping in closer.

"I know," I said, determined.

"You are in love with one," he said with a mischievous grin.

"I know, but he's different."

"From me?" Jagger brushed my hair away from my neck.

I stepped back, bumping into my chair. "From the typical vampire," I said sharply.

Jagger laughed, having fun with his little game. "Well . . . you seemed to blend in with the Dungeon," he said, confronting me again. "And that Phoenix guy."

I placed the chair between us, not saying anything. I didn't like what he was insinuating, that I was attracted to Phoenix—someone other than my boyfriend—even though the reality was that Phoenix *was* Alexander.

"How can you be in love with a vampire and not want to have a club where he can attend?"

"You know I mean nefarious, unknown vampires."

"Do I really? You think Alexander is the only benevolent vampire?"

"Uh . . . no."

"Or are you afraid that if he spends enough time around his kind, he might prefer their company?" he asked, putting his foot on the chair and leaning in. "He might be reminded of what he is missing."

That was something I hadn't imagined. I had only been thinking about two things—the potential danger of vampires mixing with unsuspecting mortals, and the risk of blowing the coffin lid off of the secret identity of my boyfriend, thus threatening his stay in Dullsville.

"Aren't you jealous of Luna?" Jagger asked coldly. "Don't you think it's weird—Sebastian meets her and within an hour takes the extra plunge, so to speak? And Alexander has known you for how long now?"

"It's different, and you know that. I'm not a vampire. Luna is."

"So she is," he said. "Lucky Luna. So what kind of vampire would you be? The Sebastian kind? Or the Alexander kind?"

"I came here to help, not to discuss my boyfriend."

"For which club? The mortal one, or the vampire one?" he asked. "I find it curious—perhaps more than a coincidence—that Scarlet, Onyx, and Sebastian have been suggesting a mortals-only club. You didn't happen to talk to them as well, did you?"

I wasn't about to admit that I had. "But they're right. This town is too small for an increased vampire population. Gossip spreads so quickly here. If the mortal patrons know it is safe, they will want to come. But if they get wind of anything nefarious, then they will want to shut down your club completely."

"You don't seem the type to worry about what others think."

"I worry about what their actions can do to my friends. More vampires in this town—ones not so benign, such as yourself—" I said for good measure "—can undermine or even threaten the existence of the ones who already live here."

"Alexander—"

"And now you, Luna, Sebastian, Onyx, and Scarlet."

He stood up and thought for a moment as he put the

chair back by the table. "But it seems to me that you would want this to be a place for you—to hang out with the ones you really want to be with," he said. "Really want to *be*."

I fantasized for a moment, imagined myself immersed in a world of vampires, dancing and sipping blood-filled drinks. It was an eye into the Underworld that I wouldn't get by attending Dullsville High but only by partying with vampires and being accepted as one of their own.

"I know . . . but a club full of and attracting more vampires is not good for everyone else. My parents—my brother. The townspeople."

"They'll never know we're here. Unless you tell them."

"I'm not going to tell anyone." I was miffed that he'd even insinuate that I'd be a blabbermouth after I'd kept the biggest secret from anyone—that my boyfriend was a vampire.

"I think it's risky enough as it is—with all of you hiding out in this factory it raises suspicion and fuels gossip. I don't think it's a good idea to add to the mix by inviting new vampires."

"Then what's the point of the club? What kind of business would I be running? Besides, I have a few things planned for this club to make it even more special."

"What do you mean?"

"You'll find out soon enough."

"A mortal club would be special all on its own. I don't think you truly understand how amazing it would be for us to have a place to dance," I said. "There isn't one here. Nothing for anyone to do. And you'd still make a fortune.

There's a lot of extra money these kids in town are willing to spend. Why would you want anything to get in the way of that?"

"I'm not sure I like people telling me what to do," he said, getting in my face. "Especially people who want to be a member of this club—for eternity."

I'd pushed Jagger too far.

"Does Alexander know you're here?" he asked.

"Yes, I do," he said from behind me.

I was as startled as Jagger was. I whipped around to find Alexander standing next to me.

"You wouldn't want anything to jeopardize our truce, would you?" Jagger asked.

"And I'm sure you wouldn't as well," Alexander shot back.

The tension was thick. I wasn't sure which vampire was going to budge first.

Jagger softened. "Your girlfriend was just convincing me how she could help me out."

I turned to Alexander, awaiting his reaction. I wasn't about to let on to Jagger that I hadn't told Alexander yet about assisting him in fixing up the club.

"Yes, I think it's a good idea for her to help decorate," he said.

Jagger was pleased. He had two antagonists all at once interested in his endeavor.

"Here, let me show you around," he said proudly. "With the girls pitching in and cooperation from my suppliers for the Coffin Club, this club will be up and running in a few weeks. It doesn't take any time to set up a rave—all you need is music and a place to invite people. But I want this to be more than a simple place to party. I want it to be a place to belong.

"We'll have a stage, a dance floor, a bar, and as the club expands, so will we," Jagger said, giving us a tour of the factory and his vision of the Crypt.

"What is this door to?" I asked, moving to a door on the far side of the room and twisting the knob. I'd seen on the blueprints that it led to the Covenant. It was locked.

"Nothing," he said, guiding me away.

Perhaps Jagger had had a change of heart. With Sebastian, me, and now Alexander on board and telling him not to invite more vampires to Dullsville, he might not want anything to jeopardize his success.

"So you aren't planning on spreading word about the club to vampires?" Alexander asked.

"I think Raven's right," Jagger replied. "Why shouldn't I fill the club with mortals?" he said with a wicked grin.

I wasn't sure if I'd really convinced him or not. But especially now that Jagger had explained the plans for the Crypt, I really couldn't wait until it opened.

"I'm glad you'll be part of the club," Jagger said. "You will be the first on the invitation list, Raven. I wouldn't want it any other way."

9 Freak Factory

As soon as the torture of another dreadfully monotonous Dullsville High day was over, I raced to the Sinclair Mill. Nothing was going to stop me from helping Jagger and his cryptic clique from decorating the decadent dance club. When I made my way inside the decaying building I saw that Jagger had already marked the floor with glow tape where the stage, dance floor, and bar would be. While the vampires slept, I swept, removed empty cardboard boxes, and cleared away any debris that would get in the way of the quick renovations. By the time the sun set and the vampires awoke, I was exhausted.

Alexander greeted me with a kiss and Javalicious coffee, and I sat on a box sipping it and watching as Onyx and Scarlet and the vampires worked. Scarlet drank her own piping hot latte. But instead of cocoa beans, hers was brewed with blood.

I rested my weary head against Alexander's shoulder. In this environment, unlike any other in Dullsville, I was accepted as one of the "in" crowd—and I was in my element—hanging out with vampires and helping decorate a nocturnal dance club. I looked on as a truck backed into a loading dock and a few guys that looked more dead than alive loaded chairs, lighting equipment, and a pool table into the factory.

Alexander kept a watchful eye on the incoming boxes, making sure that there were no nefarious items or clues about whether Jagger still planned on opening the Covenant. Sebastian did his best to help, but Luna clung to him, keeping his hands busy. He often got caught up in talking to Alexander and had to be nudged back to work by Jagger.

As the evening wore on, it was clear that there was only one person who didn't contribute to the transformation: Luna. The wispy fairy girl draped herself on a chair like a princess and, when breaks were taken, canoodled with Sebastian or asked him to fetch her bloody lattes. Several times I caught her fingering Sebastian's dreadlocks but staring at Alexander. I felt she was up to something, but what, I wasn't sure.

The following day at school, Becky and I were having lunch by the flagpole while waiting for Matt to join us. She was biting into a sandwich and I was picking at my organic peanut butter one.

"Have you heard any more about that club?" Becky asked out of the blue. "I hear rumblings all the time, but no one has any concrete information. I was wondering where it's going to be and when it's going to open."

I had to tell Becky what I knew about the club—leaving out, of course, the vampire element. The rumors about the club echoed off the walls of Dullsville High, and it wasn't right to keep her in the dark any longer.

"You have to swear to secrecy."

"Of course. You know something?"

"I know a lot."

Becky put her sandwich aside. "Tell me everything."

"It's Jagger—he's going to open a club here. And it's going to be in the vacant Sinclair Mill."

"Wow—that sounds cool."

"But you can't tell anyone because Alexander and I have to find out a bit more about it."

"Like what?"

"Like who he's opening it to."

"I thought I heard it was for everyone."

"Yes. But I want to confirm it first. And I have bigger news," I said, bursting to tell her more.

"What's bigger than that?"

"He told me I can help him!"

"That is awesome!"

"I went there yesterday and helped clean up."

"I'd love to help, too," Becky said.

I hadn't anticipated her reaction and willingness to be involved. I couldn't imagine Becky being on the inside of the factory, setting up the club with the vampires. It was one thing for me to be there—it was another for her.

"I'm not sure you'd enjoy it. It's really messy work."

"And working on a farm isn't?"

She had a point. "It's just that—"

"I usually have all my homework done by the end of the day," she said. "So I could use the time after school to help you guys."

"Well, they really don't start working until the evening. And they go all night, since they don't have school."

"I can help then, too. Matt is so busy with his scrimmages. It would be good for me to have something to do besides always waiting on the sidelines." Becky flashed her soft baby face and sweet pleading eyes.

"Fine," I said. "But this is our secret. I'm going over there tonight with Alexander. We'll pick you up on the way."

Just then Matt bolted out of the main entrance and headed over to us.

"My lips are sealed," Becky said with a wink.

Becky dug her powder blue nails into my arm as I led her down the dark gravel road toward the factory.

"This mill is so creepy," she said. Her teeth were chattering, not from the cold but from fear. "I can't imagine anyone would want to come here willingly. I'm glad I'm not meeting you here."

"I'd never do that to you," I said.

"Why don't they have lights inside?" she asked, looking at the darkened building as we walked to the door of the factory. "I only see flickering candles."

"I guess the electricity doesn't work yet."

To me this was like a dream place; to my best friend it was a nightmare. She cowered, several times covering her hair as if at any moment a swarm of bats would fly over her head. She might have been right.

Alexander opened the unwieldy door.

"Are you sure this is safe?" Becky asked before stepping inside.

"I wouldn't bring you here if it wasn't." I took her hand. "I won't let anything happen to you," I said.

She seemed a bit relieved, but only slightly, when we entered the factory and it was illuminated with votives and candelabras.

"I'm trying to be brave," she said as she maneuvered around an empty crate.

Her foot hit something as we walked.

"Yikes!" she said with a gasp. "What's that? I'm afraid to look. Is it a dead body?"

"It's just an empty crate," I assured her.

She wasn't about to let go of my hand. I was touched that she was battling her fears to share in my new hangout.

There was an awkward pause when we entered the main room and I saw Jagger seated on a bar stool. When he spotted us, he immediately rose. He was surprised, and, by his frown, I could see he was not too happy that I'd brought a visitor.

"She's with us," I said. "She's not going to spoil your secret."

There was an even more awkward pause when Sebastian spotted Becky.

It was obvious he still had a pang for her—and more

so since he'd tasted her blood.

Becky appeared delighted to see Sebastian, and the two locked eyes.

Luna swooped in from the shadows, sensing their romantic tension, and grabbed Sebastian around his waist as if he were a prize she'd won at a state fair.

"Sebastian and I were just thinking of ways to promote the club," Luna proclaimed. "We thought about T-shirts. I was thinking mine could say WELCOME TO THE CRYPT and on the back SEBASTIAN'S GHOUL."

"That sounds awesome," I said.

"We brought Raven's best friend, Becky," Alexander said. "She wanted to help out."

Alexander's words were like a knight's to his round table. His permission for Becky to be there wasn't going to be challenged by anyone. Not even Jagger.

Sebastian squirmed in Luna's clutches. It was apparent he was trying to finagle his position so he could talk to Becky. But Luna wasn't going to let my best friend intercept her new boyfriend's attention.

Luna grabbed his hand. "Jagger needs these crates returned to the dock. And while we are there, there's something I want to show you." She flipped back her hair from her neck, exposing a tiny bite mark. She giggled and flashed her glistening lashes.

Becky wasn't suspicious. In the dim light of the mill, the marks were not clearly visible and could have been just a scratch. But I knew their true origin.

"Yes, Sebastian and I have big plans for the club, and

for us. Right, Sabby?" Luna said.

"Sabby?" I mouthed to Alexander.

"We are going to be together for a while," she said, then whispered so only I could hear, "maybe even eternity."

I wasn't sure why she was trying to shove her relationship with Sebastian in front of me and Alexander. Perhaps she was still hurt by Alexander's spurning her at the covenant ceremony in Romania. Perhaps she was still in love with him and wanted to show him what he was missing. Or maybe she wanted to make me feel bad because I didn't have what she did—a guy who bit her. Most likely, it was all of the above.

"Uh—" Sebastian said as he attempted to make conversation with us, but Luna's charms were no match for him, and he was reluctantly led away by the tempting vampire.

I proudly showed Becky around the room and described the plans to her.

Alexander watched as the two of us made our way to each corner. I could feel his gaze on me, and I sensed an ease on his part that I was truly happy with this cryptic endeavor.

"Here's where the dance floor is going to be," I said. "And here there are going to be cages."

"How cool!" Becky said. "I can't imagine dancing in a cage, but I've seen it on TV."

She took out her cell phone from her purse.

"Strike a pose," she said, holding up her phone as a camera.

I laughed and raised my arms like I owned the club myself.

We had to get out of the way as a few workers came through with large wooden panels. She snapped a few photos of them and they appeared shocked, as if no one had taken their picture before.

Becky continued taking pictures of Jagger's workers as they placed cardboard tombstones against a wall.

"You shouldn't do that—" I said to her as they winced from the flash of light.

"What's that?" Jagger asked, storming in the room. When he saw Becky taking pictures, he snapped. "You can't do that! Not here!"

Becky's cheery face turned sour. She was taken off guard, and I could tell she felt awful.

"She didn't mean anything by it," I said, facing Jagger.

Sebastian must have heard Jagger's harsh tone, as he and Luna came running into the room.

"Becky was taking pictures of the workers!" Jagger said. "This is why—"

"She didn't do anything wrong." I defended her. "I asked her to take those."

I could see Becky's cheeks getting redder. I'd brought her here, and within five minutes she was being insulted.

"What's the big deal?" she asked softly.

"I don't allow cameras in the club," Jagger said.

"I'm sorry. I didn't know. I was just going to take some action shots," Becky said innocently. "Before and after pictures."

"I think that's a great idea," Sebastian said.

Luna huffed. "You do?" She folded her arms defiantly, clearly miffed.

"Jagger is so secretive about this place because he has a lot invested in it, and he's afraid of people hearing about it before it's finished," I said.

"I'm not going to show the pictures to anyone," Becky whimpered.

"I know," I said. "Jagger just overreacted."

Jagger sidled up to Becky. I was ready to pounce if he did anything nefarious to my best friend. By the look of it so were Alexander and Sebastian. They were suddenly at my best friend's side.

Jagger wasn't about to take us on and instead changed his tune. "How about you take a few of Raven by the tombstones?" he suggested. "I'd love to have some of them. And I think your idea about before and after shots is really creative."

We were impressed with Jagger's handling of the situation.

Luna wasn't as much. She didn't like Sebastian's sudden defense of Becky and was obviously threatened.

"I don't have to, really," Becky said. She began putting her phone in her pocket when Jagger stopped her.

"No, I think it's a great idea. I wish I'd thought of it myself. Besides, Raven loves to be photographed," Jagger said. "The others? Not so much. We aren't as photogenic."

"Thanks, Jagger," I said.

"Yes, thanks!" Becky said. "I can be the official photographer of the Crypt."

"Awesome!" Jagger said. "You'll have to send me the shots."

"I'll make you a scrapbook."

Jagger seemed genuinely pleased with Becky's enthusiasm and naiveté.

Becky was so excited about her new role at the Crypt. She began staging and snapping pictures of me as furniture and fixtures were being loaded into the mill.

Sebastian, Luna, Alexander, and Jagger remained aloof so as not to be a part of any of the photos.

I'd never been so happy—save for being on the other end of Alexander's lips or cuddling together in his coffin. Here I was with my best friend and true love, surrounded by modern-day vampires and creating a haunting dance club.

Even Onyx and Scarlet were taking to my best friend.

"Here," Onyx said, extending her hand. "I'll take some of you and Raven together."

Becky and I posed by the tombstones while Onyx snapped pictures of us.

As Onyx returned the phone to Becky, Scarlet was at the bar, pouring blood-red liquid into a cup.

"What's that?" Becky asked.

"Uh . . . Kool-Aid," Scarlet replied.

"I love Kool-Aid."

"I wish I had more," she said.

"But we do. In back," Onyx said without thinking.

Scarlet shot her an evil glare. Then Onyx realized her misstep and bit her burgundy-colored lip.

"That's okay," I said. "We'll pick up something on the way home."

The last thing I needed was Becky putting a cup of blood to her mouth and taking a swig. She'd never recover. And neither would I.

Becky stood out like a daisy in a sea of dead roses in her cheery colors, while we were dark in our morbid outfits.

"So where are you guys staying?" Becky asked.

"Here," Scarlet said as if Becky already knew.

"In this place?" Becky was as shocked as she was horrified.

"Uh-huh." Scarlet grinned.

"There's barely any electricity. And there's no furniture."

"We know," Scarlet said.

"Why don't you stay with one of the families in town? Or at least a hotel?"

"It's free here, and besides, we like it," Onyx said.

"This place isn't acceptable for you guys to sleep in. We have some extra room at our house," Becky said. "I can check with my parents, but I'm sure you're more than welcome to stay—"

"That is so sweet of you," Scarlet said sincerely.

"I hate to think of you sleeping here with the bugs and spiders," she said, shuddering.

"We like it that way," Scarlet insisted.

"I think they're lucky," I chimed in with a smile.

"Of course you would." Becky laughed. "It's like Camp Raven. You guys are so brave," Becky went on. "Where do you sleep?"

"Downstairs."

"Ooh . . .," Becky said. "You must be scared to death—at night."

"Actually it's during the day we are creeped out," Scarlet said.

The two vampires giggled.

"I can show you," Onyx said.

Scarlet cleared her throat. I imagined Onyx opening the door revealing five coffin beds. If Becky didn't faint, I would.

Onyx was a gothic version of Becky. She was as sincere as she was kind. At the end of the day, though she was a vampire, she didn't have bite.

Just then Alexander came and got us.

"Jagger could use some help painting the entrance."

"Now, that's something I can do," Becky said eagerly. "Sleep in a factory's basement, no, but paint a factory wall, yes."

The following day Becky was a little preoccupied. I didn't get to the bottom of it until after school when I tried to make plans with her to go back to the factory.

"I need to do some homework," she said as we headed for her truck. "I can drop you off at home."

"I thought you'd already finished it."

"I did . . . but I think I should probably look it over again. Just to make sure."

Becky was an amateur at lying and a novice at fibbing. Her excuses were transparent.

"You don't want to go?" I fished.

"Do I have to? I know I said I wanted to help, and I do. But do I have to go back into that place before it's finished?"

"Of course not . . . I just thought—"

"I can shop for you guys. I can hand out flyers. And when it's finished, I'd love to go. But now? Without proper lighting and cleaning . . ."

"Don't worry."

"I didn't sleep at all last night. I kept thinking about how dark and spooky it was there—so much so that I started seeing shadows in my room. And Scarlet, Onyx, and Luna—I don't think it's safe that they sleep there."

"Relax," I said. "Why don't you stay home and work on the scrapbook then."

Becky sighed like a yoga instructor. The sullen expression she'd worn all day drew back, a cheery smile overcame her, and her cheeks blossomed apple red.

I, too, felt elated, until Trevor jumped between me and the truck.

"Where are you going in such a hurry?" he asked.

"I don't remember it being any of your business."

"You wouldn't be snooping, would you? To find out where that club is going to be located?"

"Maybe I already know. Besides, how would you know?"

"Things like permits to vacant buildings need to be cleared first. And those things don't come to just anyone. My dad owns this town and everything in it."

He guided my hair off my shoulder and I batted him away.

"Not everything!" I said. "He doesn't own me."

"Not yet," he said with a grin. "But I can ensure you full access to the club—and to something else."

"You?" I laughed out loud.

"No, something that you really want." He held up a key and dangled it in front of my face.

Then he slid the key in his back pocket. "Want to get it?"

"Not in this lifetime!" I opened the truck door and hopped inside.

The front door to the factory was an unwieldy door that couldn't hold a lock even if there was one on it. Besides, it would be just as easy to pull the frail door off its hinges. If Trevor had a key to a door inside the Crypt, what did it lead to?

Trevor watched me as Becky drove off. He was gorgeous and menacing, and was one step ahead of me. It only made him more annoying.

I arrived at the mill just after sunset. Jagger was right— there wasn't much to do to make the abandoned mill a place to have a rave. Just clear boxes and add some lighting. But Jagger had bigger dreams for his parties. He wanted the patrons to be comfortable and have a unique experience.

The transformation was shocking. A bar was placed in the middle of the northern-most wall. Several round tables, wooden chairs, and bar stools were covered with black velvet. It was truly magical how much they were able to do under the cloak of darkness.

I beamed with excitement as the abandoned factory was becoming the ultimate dance club.

I found Sebastian and Luna overlapping limbs on a crate in the corner. It was obvious that with Luna around, Sebastian wasn't being the help to Jagger that Jagger was hoping for.

"Luna, maybe you and Raven could get us some food at that diner," Jagger said. "Take my car," he said, throwing the keys to his sister.

Luna and I each tried to hide our reluctance. For both of us, it meant time away from our loves. And worse, time together.

Each vampire looked at us, seeing our reactions and waiting to see which one of us came up with an excuse first.

"Sure," Luna finally said. "Let's go."

It was a thrill to ride in Jagger's hearse. A plastic skeleton hung from the rearview mirror and the vintage car's interior was perfectly amazing, with restored black vinyl upholstered seats.

The black curtains in back were drawn closed, and I wondered if indeed there might be a body in the hearse. The silver bat hood ornament glistened in the moonlight.

Luna's candy-pink-nailed fingers gripped the black leather steering wheel and her hair cascaded over her shoulders as if she were on a photo shoot.

"So what are your plans?" I asked, trying to pry any info out of her while I had the chance.

"Building the Crypt."

"And who do you think will show up?" I asked.

"I don't know. I'm sure Jagger has it all figured out."

"You mean you don't know?"

"Know what?"

"Is it going to be like the Coffin Club, with an underground vampire hangout?"

Just then she pulled into the parking lot.

She withdrew a list from her purse.

"You didn't answer—"

She got out of the car and surveyed the list like she was memorizing it for a quiz. She didn't even look up and continued to walk through the parking lot, ignoring impending traffic.

"Watch out, Luna," I said when a car came too close for my comfort.

"What?" she said indifferently, reaching the curb and entering the restaurant.

When we stepped into Hatsy's Diner, all heads turned. Moms and dads gave us the look of "don't grow up to look like them, sweetie."

And though the guys in town preferred their girls in paisley, it didn't stop them from gawking at the new girl in ripped tights and a skirt that barely covered her bottom.

I was invisible as far as they were concerned.

No one ever paid attention to me, but when Luna arrived at the counter, more than three waiters came over to help. She leaned over the counter and gave the soda jerk our order.

He quickly passed it back to the cooks and raced around to the shake machine.

Luna got bored and turned to me.

"So, what do you think of my new boyfriend?" she said with sappy eyes.

I didn't want to tell her the truth and risk being mean. I thought Sebastian was great—but not for her.

"He's so funny and handsome," she gushed. "The best of both worlds." She twisted her hair between her fingers. "He's going to take me to Paris and Rome. What about Alexander? Where is he taking you?"

Alexander hadn't taken me anywhere—and we didn't have plans to go anywhere.

"We talk about Rome and Paris, too," I said. "But we are far too busy for any of that right now," I shot back.

"Oh yes, you are bogged down by school. I don't know how you manage."

I don't, I wanted to say.

"I think I might want to stay here with Sebastian."

"He's staying here?"

"For now. So I will, too."

"For how long?" I asked.

"As long as it takes."

"As long as what takes?"

She wasn't about to answer. Luna had coyness down to a science.

"So, when do you think Alexander will turn you?" she said directly.

It was the one question that burned inside of me. I wasn't about to tell her that. She already knew.

"Do you know—his grandmother was never bitten. You could become just like her. In that monument in the cemetery."

I was thrown by her statement. It was so harsh and brutal that I was taken off guard. I was mad for me—but even more mad for Alexander's grandmother.

But then I thought about what it meant—if that was my fate, too. And if it was, it wasn't so bad. Many people live their entire lives never finding true love. Grandmother Sterling had loved and had a wonderful family. And I had found true love at sixteen.

"It's a shame," Luna continued, "his grandfather died before they could make that decision."

"But if he was a vampire . . ." I asked, surprised, "then how could he die?"

"There was a revolt. Decades ago. Vampires can die, too, you know. It's hard, but they can. And it's not a pleasant way to go."

This was information I hadn't heard from Alexander. There were rumors of a revolt in Romania and how that was the reason the baroness had built the Mansion on Benson Hill. But I thought it was just a rumor.

"She came here to protect her family," Luna went on.

"Was it your family that started the revolt?" I asked cautiously.

"No . . ." She laughed with a cute cackle. "It was mortals. They are far more destructive than vampires. I thought you would have figured that out by now."

She drew a long sip from her strawberry-pink shake.

"But is that what you really want? To spend your life waiting? It seems so pathetic."

Her sharp words pierced me more painfully than fangs.

"Well, I'll be sure to invite you to our wedding," she continued.

"Wedding?" I asked.

"Yes, when Sebastian and I get married."

"You are getting married? But you just met. And you're not even . . ."

"I'm eighteen. Romeo and Juliet betrothed their love at sixteen. And no, we aren't getting married today. But eventually. I'm sure Alexander is kicking himself, seeing all he could have had that his best friend has now. A partnership in a club. And a girl who isn't afraid to be bitten."

"I don't know what you're talking about. I'm not afraid."

"Aren't you? It seems like you are waiting an eternity—for eternity."

"You don't know anything about it," I said through gritted teeth.

"So if you both are so serious and so in love, then when is your official date?"

She knew what Alexander was like. She knew he wasn't going to turn me anytime soon, and she was shoving it in my face.

"We don't need that to show how much we care for each other."

"Those are just excuses. Commitment. That's what it's all about. Taking that covenant together. Bonding yourselves together for eternity. Isn't that what we are all looking for? Maybe Alexander wasn't ready to do that with me, but it's obvious he isn't ready to do that with you, either."

Now I was boiling mad. I felt like dumping my shake on her head right in front of the whole town. Anger welled up in my boots all the way through my torn tights and raged up my spine.

"Eternity is forever, but marriage? That's even longer," she said with that cute girlie giggle.

"What if I told you that Alexander planned to turn me? On my twenty-first birthday. In the cemetery, in front of the whole town!"

"Then I'd tell you I think you're making it up."

I fumed inside.

"Besides, we can ask Alexander all about that turning at twenty-one when we get back."

I was horrified at the thought of returning to the factory and Luna asking Alexander about something we hadn't really discussed and I had just now made up.

"And I'll ask Sebastian about your wedding, too," I shot back.

Luna froze, frostier than her pink shake. It was then I knew I'd caught her, too.

"Well, for now, we'll just consider our discussion a secret between friends."

The waiter placed two large bags of food and a carton filled with shakes on the counter. Luna grabbed a handful of napkins and her shake and headed out the door and left me to struggle with the rest.

When we arrived back at the mill, I bolted out the car door, leaving Luna to carry the load. Only it backfired. No one was glad to see me. The vampires were hungry and she got the credit for the bounty.

Each ravenous vampire took his or her meal and tore into the food while I picked at mine, having eaten three times that day already.

It was very obvious that Sebastian was head-over–Doc Martens for Luna. He doted on her so much it made my stomach turn. I knew he was mesmerized by her, as she did have a hypnotic glow around her. However, if Alexander wasn't interested in her, then I wondered why I was so jealous of her.

Scarlet also seemed preoccupied. I sensed a loneliness emanating from her. We all were coupled up. There were obviously three couples here—Luna and Sebastian, Alexander and me, Jagger and Onyx—and each couple was in a stage of romance, whether one had been bitten or not. And there was one single vampire girl. Scarlet, however, longed for a mortal just as I did for a vampire. She was pining for Trevor, a conservative mortal who was a player on and off the field. I knew Trevor wasn't good for her, for so many reasons. And at the end of the day, if he was going to be with his antithesis girl, someone goth, it probably would have been me.

The advantage I had was the sunlight. Something Scarlet, oddly enough, longed for, and I detested.

Instead of giving me a good-night kiss at my front door, Alexander came inside. I think we both needed some private time together since all our nights were being consumed with the Crypt and being on the watch for the possible Covenant. Alexander didn't hang out in my bedroom a lot.

I preferred the Mansion, with its magnificent space and style, and it was also minus two doting parents and one pesky little brother.

But having Alexander in my room felt amazing. My little space didn't seem so morbid after all. Alexander brought life to it. And having him there was exhilarating. The way he walked around, examining and touching everything on display, was like he was touching me. I watched him look closely at my knickknacks, books, and music as if he was trying to get to know me or see into my soul. I felt safe with him here. Nothing could bother me—not physically or emotionally. And as tough as I was, it was nice for a moment to let my guard down and feel safe because of someone else for a change.

Alexander sat on my bed, like a gentleman would, if it were acceptable for a gentleman to sit on a lady's bed. But I pulled him over and made him lie beside me. I imagined what it would be like if he could cuddle with me as I fell asleep here, just as I did with him in his coffin. But that wasn't going to happen anytime soon, especially when we'd often get interrupted by Billy Boy, looking for attention.

"Wow—I don't know how you sleep like this. I worry about you all the time," he said tenderly.

"What do you mean?"

"Open—exposed. Anyone—or anything—could come into your room. You aren't hidden from danger."

"What would come into my room?"

"I don't even want to think about it. I'm miles away from you and . . . it's just not safe. Not from the sun, I mean. But from people. There are so many things that can happen if you're not secured."

"We have a security system." I caressed his hair playfully, but Alexander was serious.

"I know. But don't you feel strange looking up and knowing anyone could watch you sleeping? Especially since you can't see in the dark."

I thought about it for a moment. I'd contemplated many things from the vampire's viewpoint, but this was something I hadn't.

"I didn't mean to scare you. It's one of the reasons I want to . . ."

"Yes?"

"It is one of the reasons I'd want you to be a vampire."

I sat up. "Really?"

"It just seemed odd to me that mortals would prefer to sleep that way."

"That's not what I meant." I leaned into him eagerly.

"I just feel funny—you here, not totally secured. But I guess it works for your kind. It always has."

"Yes, but back to what you were saying." I hoped he'd go back to talking about me becoming a vampire.

"I want you to be safe, that's all," he said, squeezing my hand.

From Alexander's perspective, we mortals lived open, vulnerable lives. He was hidden away from the sun and predators. Even if someone were to find the coffin, he was locked inside.

"It's weird. You can see all these things and hear all

these noises. No wonder you have insomnia."

"I have insomnia because you aren't here with me. So . . . if you really want me to be safe, maybe it's time."

"I'd just feel safer if you'd start sleeping in a coffin."

Just then my door creaked open.

Billy's expression turned to surprise.

"Get out!" I said, hopping off the bed. "Uh . . . we are making up lyrics to a song."

But that didn't keep Billy out. Instead he was totally interested.

"You're writing a song? That's so cool. I want to hear it."

"It goes, 'Safer in a coffin, and if your brother doesn't leave, he'll be in one, too.'"

Billy just frowned.

"It's okay, man," Alexander said. "What's up?"

"What are you doing in my room?" I snarled at Billy. "I'm one step away from bringing back Nerd Boy."

My brother wasn't bothered by my threat. He was under the Alexander spell. Like a kid in the company of a professional athlete, Billy was enamored by Alexander's presence. Alexander was the big brother Billy never had. And in kind, Alexander was always attentive to my brother, as kind and focused on him as he could be.

"Isn't it past your bedtime?" I finally asked.

I could see Alexander had a longing for my younger sibling, as if he was missing one himself. He seemed delighted by the attention.

I let the two talk for a few more minutes before I led, or rather pushed, my little brother out of my room. Alexander and I had enough distractions to deal with and I wanted my precious alone time with him.

I thought now would be a good time to bring up what I'd learned from my conversation with Luna at Hatsy's Diner. I sat on the bed with Alexander and entwined my fingers with his. "Sebastian really likes Luna," I said.

"Yes, I can see that."

"No. I mean they've talked future and everything."

"Yeah . . . ?"

"I think they are going to get married."

Alexander laughed. "Sebastian? I don't think so."

"Luna seems to think so. And the way he drools all over her, I wouldn't be surprised. . . ."

"You don't know Sebastian that well then." Alexander continued to laugh.

"Well, maybe he found the right one," I said.

"For today."

"I think this is different," I tried to tell him.

"How?"

"Because he bit her." I looked him straight in the eyes. But Alexander wasn't impressed.

"But didn't he say the same thing about Becky? That she was different?" Alexander asked.

"I guess . . ."

"Do you know how many times I've heard him say that?" Alexander said with a grin. "That's what vampires do, they bite."

"But you don't."

"Not yet . . ." He lifted my hair from my neck and

nibbled it, sending me into giggles.

Then he took my hand. "Sebastian's only heard me say I was in love once. About a girl I met when I came to this town."

My heart melted. Alexander was truly dreamy. His soulful eyes stared into mine and I kissed him with all my love.

When we finished our embrace, I thought again about our conversation. "But with Luna—Sebastian seems to be sure this time," I said. "And he's acting on it—though impulsively," I lamented.

"Raven, I don't live my life based on what everyone else is doing. I never have. And I thought you didn't either. That's one of the reasons I'm so attracted to you."

He was right. Why did I have to live my life differently— or expect things for Alexander and me because of any-one else? I'd been living according to my rules since I was born. And now, because Luna came to town, I was going to adjust my whole existence to keep up with hers? And worse, I was trying to do the same for Alexander.

But I couldn't get past her. She struck me to the core. It wasn't rational but emotional.

"It's normal to be jealous sometimes," Alexander said. "But what are you jealous of, really? A guy who meets a girl and, without a thought, bites her at a party? What if Sebastian goes to another party? How will she feel then?"

I guess I was jealous that Luna was a vampire and I was still a mortal. That she was bitten and I wasn't. And that she thought she was getting married . . . and I still wasn't sure. But was I brave enough to say all those things to Alexander? To confront him out of fear and not out of love? And because of one impulsive person and another shifty one, to make him prove things to me he might not be ready to prove?

Alexander pulled me to him and took my face into his hands. "I hope that biting you isn't the only way I can convince you of my love for you. It's not that I don't want to. And it's not that I don't think about it every day. I've loved you from the first moment I saw you."

He stared so deeply into my eyes that I could see myself in them. For a moment, I was saddened, realizing he couldn't see his own reflection in mine. And if I was turned, I wouldn't be able to see myself in his anymore.

But not seeing reflections didn't seem to bother him. He wasn't asking me to change. He loved me the way I was, and no guy had ever done that before.

He drew my face to his and kissed me deeply, kissed the jealousy away, and I was flooded with a sense of love and an even deeper eternal desire.

11

Buzz Kill

Jagger asked us to meet the following night not at the Crypt but at the soccer field. It was an odd sight, to say the least: a bunch of vampires hanging out on the bleachers at Trevor's soccer game. I would have loved to have hung out at the Crypt, but it was Jagger's plan for the girls to get out and drum up buzz for the club.

Luna had her hand on Sebastian's leg the entire time, but it was clear to me that she was staring at Alexander. I wondered deep down if she was involved with Sebastian to get back at or to get close to Alexander. But Alexander didn't appear to care or even notice. He had his arm around me and was as captivated with the game as any one of Dullsville's students was.

Becky seemed to be preoccupied with her phone and occasionally glanced at Sebastian.

Scarlet beamed. Her face flushed to match her dyed

hair. She honed in on Trevor and, as much as it turned my stomach to see her lust after my nemesis, I was moved that she was so happy to watch Trevor.

"I'd like some popcorn and a drink," Luna directed Sebastian with a flirty gaze. Back in Romania, Luna had grown up as a mortal, and a very popular one at that. Soccer games were nothing new to her.

While I sat with Onyx and Scarlet, Becky stood at the edge of the bleachers holding her cell phone.

"Who are you texting?" I asked her. "I'm here and Matt's on the field."

"I'm not texting."

"Then what are you doing?"

"I never got that picture of Sebastian. And since this isn't the Crypt, I can take as many pics as I want. I'd like to add it to the scrapbook for Jagger."

I rose. I didn't know what to do. She had her camera poised and aimed at Sebastian.

"I don't think—" I said. But it was too late. I heard the *click click click* and saw flashes as she snapped away.

Onyx and Scarlet must have noticed, too, as they whispered together.

Becky returned triumphant. "I made sure I saved them this time. Let's take a look at them," she said.

"Hey—watch Matt," I said. "He's on his way to scoring! Maybe you should be paying attention to him and not Sebastian," I hinted. "I think he's working extra hard for you."

"Really?" she asked. She watched her boyfriend as he

ran down the field, kicking the soccer ball. "Go, Matt, go!"

Becky forgot about her pictures and for the rest of the game was entranced by Matt's athletic abilities.

After the game, Prada-bees inched away from us, and we got a ton of stares. But when Trevor, sweaty and charged up from a win, came and talked to Jagger, and he hung out for a few minutes with the soccer team, the onlookers gawked even more. But when they noticed that Trevor liked these goths, then they looked at them like there must have been something worthwhile about them—like a new purse from an up-and-coming designer.

It was the first time in my existence in Dullsville that I wasn't the only outsider. I was in a crowd of girls and guys and it looked like I belonged to their club.

The next day, after last bell, I headed to my locker to find Trevor leaning against it.

"I bet it breaks your heart to have two of your friends pine for me the way they do," he said proudly. "Luna . . . and now Scarlet. They can't keep their hands off of me."

"It's just because you are foreign to them. It's like if they went to the zoo and stared at the monkeys. You are the monkey."

Trevor broke a smile.

The more I pushed his buttons, the more he loved it. He stepped aside, but not without brushing against me. He peered over me as I unlocked my locker and opened its door.

"So what about that key?" I asked.

"I knew you'd be asking me about it sooner or later." He pulled the cord out from underneath his shirt and dangled the key in front of me.

"What do you want for it?" I sneered. "Five dollars?"

"I don't want money," he said with a wicked grin.

"What does it go to?"

"A kiss will unlock more than this key will," he whispered in my ear.

Steam burned inside me. Maybe the key didn't even go to anything. Maybe it was just something Trevor made up. And I would be the fool once again.

But what if I was wrong, and perhaps it was important. Maybe it was the key to unlocking something magical in the factory that held the answers Jagger was keeping secret.

"What's going on?" Becky asked, puzzled by Trevor's proximity to me.

"Raven and I were just having a chat. But it's time to go. You know where you can find me," Trevor said. "You have my number."

"The hazmat crew removed it for me."

Becky looked at me as Trevor walked away. "What was that all about?"

"Same bully, different bullying," I said. Then I changed the topic to something more exciting. "I've been so busy but I wanted to talk about something with you. I want to get a present for Alexander's birthday. Something really special. But I don't live in New York or L.A. What can I get him here that he'll like?"

"He loves art," she said.

"Yes . . . but I can't draw or paint. And I can't afford anything worth having."

"And you."

"Aww. That's so sweet!" I beamed at my best friend's compliment. "But guys are so hard to buy for. We always get my dad golf or tennis stuff. But Alexander doesn't play sports. And I don't know what kind of supplies he needs. Besides, that doesn't seem fun."

"I get Matt computer sports games. But I suppose Alexander's not into that."

"I was thinking about surprising him with a nice intimate dinner. Just us in his backyard. Or at the cemetery."

"That sounds very romantic!"

But I wanted to give him something unique—after all, he was one of a kind. But what does one give to someone of the Underworld?

It was then I knew. My blood. In a vial. For a vampire, it was the ultimate gift.

"I have it!" But I couldn't tell her. She'd freak, just as she should, if I told her I was going to give my boyfriend a vial of my blood. But in this case it wasn't creepy. My boyfriend was a vampire.

"So what is it? What are you so excited about?"

"Uh . . . a gargoyle!"

Becky's eyes lit up. "That is the best gift for him! He will so love it! Wish I'd thought of it!"

"I'll go to Annie's Antiques to shop."

"I'll go with you. I might find a gargoyle for Matt, too."

I shot her a puzzled expression. "Fine. I'd love to have the company."

We headed to the antique store that I frequented and I immediately scanned the glass case for a vial. There were many crystals and gems, but at first glance I didn't see a vial.

"A gargoyle isn't going to be in the case, silly," Becky said, standing by the outdoor figurines. "They'll be over here."

"Yes, I know."

I glanced back at the case and saw a shiny vial. It was small, with a sterling silver serpent winding around it and a small hook. I could string some cord through it and it would be the ultimate gift for my vampire boyfriend.

I checked the price tag and I had enough money to buy it.

"Here's one." Becky pulled me away from the case and toward the gargoyle.

"That is cool," I said. "But it's out of my price range."

I didn't have enough for both the gargoyle and the present I most wanted to get. I wasn't sure how to conceal that I wanted to get a vial.

"Oh, yes," Becky said. "It is kind of steep."

Instead I decided to make my gift choice known—but not the reason. "I want to buy this," I said, returning to the case and pointing out the vial. "It's really cool."

"I thought you wanted a gargoyle," she said, peering in the case. "What's he going to do with a vial?"

"I could put something special in it."

"A potion?" she teased.

"Yes, exactly. A love potion."

"But he doesn't need that—he already loves you. I think he'd like a gargoyle much better. But he's your boyfriend."

Annie placed the vial in a small gift box. "Would you like me to wrap it?"

"No, thank you," I said. "I'll do that at home." I couldn't tell her I still had to fill it with my blood.

Now I was just going to have to figure out how to fill it.

That evening I was rushing through dinner and scarfing down my food.

"Where are you off to in such a hurry?" my mom asked. "You've been MIA for the last several weeks."

"I'm helping some friends with a project."

"Friends? You have friends?" my brother teased.

"Yes, who are these people?" my dad asked.

"They're some new kids. I'm just helping them out."

"With a school project?" my brother asked. They all looked at me as if the situation was ridiculous.

"I'm so proud of you," my mom gushed. "See, Alexander has been good for you. You get out more, go to dances, and now are helping new students with school projects."

I couldn't break their parental hearts at this point. They were so happy with the child they thought they had. It would have been cruel to reveal the truth—that I was actually helping vampires open a club.

"Did you hear about the crop circles?" Billy asked.

"What?" I put my dinner down. Crop circles could be a bad thing.

"They were discovered this morning. They showed up on Mr. Bateman's farm."

"Are you kidding?" I asked with interrogating eyes.

"Henry and I are going to see them after dinner."

"Crop circles, here in town?" I pressed.

"Yes, aliens have arrived to take you home," he said with an obnoxious laugh only a younger brother could make.

"Billy," my dad warned in his authoritative voice.

"They're just a prank," my brother went on. "I saw how to do it on TV. It's actually really simple. All it takes is a long board and a lot of rope."

"Then maybe it was one of your nerdmates. A math club experiment," I said. "Working with diameters and circumferences. You guys are totally into that stuff."

"Me? Sneak onto someone else's property?" he said. "You think I'd do that—or any one of my friends? Trespassing—that's your expertise, not mine. Maybe you did it."

"Yes, I'm all about spending my evenings running around on a farm with a board and rope."

"Now, if they showed up at the cemetery, maybe Raven would have done it," my dad said with a chuckle. "I couldn't resist," he said, patting my hand.

I wasn't as mad at being the butt of my family's jokes as I was at Jagger's actions. When I was in Hipsterville, Jagger used crop circles to signal to vampires that it was a safe haven for them in that town, thus publicizing the invite to the Coffin Club. He was warned not to invite vampires to Dullsville, and here he was signaling them. Soon the club

116

would open and dozens of vampires could infiltrate the town.

I gulped down the rest of my dinner and headed for the Mansion. As soon as Alexander awoke I told him about the crop circles. It only took a few minutes for Alexander to get ready, and then he drove us over to Mr. Bateman's farm.

There was already a small crowd of students and townspeople there when we arrived.

The Batemans' farm was close to Becky's. Pete Bateman Senior had inherited it from his father when he retired. It stretched out at least three hundred and fifty acres and was one of the leading corn growers in Dullsville. They had a few children close to Billy Boy's age.

Pete Bateman Junior was attending to the crowd and had a metal box open on a table and his hand sticking out as each person approached the fence.

"Five dollars?" I bellowed.

"It's a deal," he said.

Pete Bateman Junior wasn't any bigger than Billy. I'd have attempted to push past him if he were my smarmy brother, but on someone else's property I'd be arrested for trespassing.

"You're charging people to see this thing?" I said in a huff. "You really can only see them from the sky," I said. "How do we know you didn't make it just as a scam?"

"You don't," he said. "Please step aside. Others are waiting."

"Don't you need a license for something like this?"

"Let the kid have his fun," Alexander said. "We'd like two, please."

"That will be ten dollars," he said.

Alexander kindly opened his wallet and handed the boy a ten-dollar bill.

"I don't know who I'm madder at now, Jagger or that Bateman kid," I said as I stormed through the cornfield.

"Calm down. Once we see it we might know better if Jagger is behind this."

As we drew near the middle of the field, we found Matt and Becky already gawking at the circle.

"I didn't expect to see you here," I said.

"My dad told us all about it," Becky said. "We had to come."

There wasn't much to do in Dullsville, so the popping up of a crop circle was a big event.

"Who or what do you think did this?" I asked.

"Maybe little Pete Bateman did it," Matt said. "He's making a killing."

"I thought so, too!" I said.

"It does seem bizarre," Becky said, squeezing Matt's hand. "I'm so weirded out."

"It's not real," I said. "I mean that an alien made it."

"What if it is?" Becky asked.

"I don't think—" I began.

"Well, you believe in vampires," she said. "Why can't I believe in aliens?"

"Because vampires don't exist," Matt said. "So you both are wrong."

But I was really right about vampires. So if I was right, did that mean maybe Becky was, too? This was one time it would have been better for the explanation to have been a landing extraterrestrial spaceship. At least it wouldn't have been caused by Jagger and his nefarious plans.

We examined the markings. "Do they look like the ones Jagger built in Hipsterville?" Alexander whispered.

"I don't know," I said in a hushed tone. "It was dark that night—like now."

"Do you remember the size?"

I shrugged my shoulders. "Do all crop circles look alike? Or are they like snowflakes?"

We stood in the middle of the field, dozens of townspeople milling about. I gazed up overhead, the stars twinkling above me. I was wondering if this was Jagger's doing when I swore I saw a bat fly past me.

"Did you see that?" I asked Alexander.

"See what?"

"It was a bat!"

He squinted but by the time I pointed in the direction, the creature was gone.

He took my hand. "I think we've seen enough. We'll have to talk to Jagger now. We have to stop him from opening the Crypt."

"Do we really?" I asked, my breath leaving my body in frustration as Alexander led me out of the cornfield.

This was one time I didn't want to follow Alexander to where he was going.

* * *

"He was with me the whole time," Onyx defended when we confronted Jagger back at the Crypt with our discovery.

"The whole time?" Alexander pressed.

"Well, most of the time," she said, resigned. "He went to Javalicious to get me coffee."

"And how long did that take?" Alexander asked.

This time Onyx didn't answer.

"But he made one of those crop circles in a cornfield near the Coffin Club," I said. "Now one shows up here, too? It can't be just coincidence."

"Yes, it can," Jagger said.

"I really don't think it was him," Onyx said.

"If she said it wasn't, then it wasn't," Scarlet said, defending her friend like I would have defended Becky.

"Were you here?" I asked cautiously. I didn't want to get into a catfight with Scarlet.

"Well . . . no," she admitted softly.

"You were with Trevor?" I asked. I shook my head.

Scarlet rose with a huff.

Jagger was offended. "You don't believe me, huh?"

"And I saw a bat," I said. "I think it was you."

Sebastian shifted back and forth uneasily.

"That was you?" Alexander asked. "You flew over the Batemans'?"

"I wanted to see what everyone was talking about," Sebastian said sheepishly.

Alexander turned his attention back to Jagger. "This club has to remain mortal. No ifs, ands, or buts."

"I don't like your tone." Jagger folded his arms.

"I don't like yours either," Alexander retorted, facing his onetime foe.

I wasn't sure if fists were going to fly.

"We can shut you down as easily as we can help you in making your club a success," Alexander threatened.

"You think I am dependent on you to make this a success?" Jagger asked.

"Bringing in unknown vampires to this town isn't good for anyone," Alexander said. "Especially you."

Suddenly Jagger was interested. "How would it bother me?" he wondered.

"What if they draw unwanted attention to us? All of a sudden hundreds of vampires descending on this town. Hanging out at Hatsy's Diner. Wandering around the cemeteries. You don't think anyone will notice?"

"They notice us enough as it is," Sebastian chimed in.

"And how do you think the town will react to this new population?" Alexander asked. "With open arms? Don't you see how Raven is treated in this town—just for the way she dresses? You think they'll embrace all these vampires you plan to have attending your underground club? You saw how careless Sebastian was. It only takes one to spoil it for the rest. Then you'll lose it all."

Sebastian scratched his dreadlocks awkwardly.

Jagger looked grim.

"But if it's just a safe dance club," Alexander went on, "that is something this town desperately needs."

Jagger's mood brightened. "And that's what I'm here to provide."

Everyone seemed skeptical of Jagger's easy change in attitude.

"How can we count on it?" Alexander asked.

"You can have my sworn oath. In blood." Jagger smiled.

Alexander paused as if he was trying to read Jagger for any underlying deception. When Jagger didn't flinch, Alexander extended his hand.

Both vampires shook on the deal.

"Now someone has to fix that crop circle," Alexander said.

"If someone flies over it—they'll be looking for your club," I told Jagger.

"Anyone in town could have done it," Jagger said.

"Well, we know one person in town who is going to fix it," Alexander responded emphatically.

Jagger rose and picked up his keys.

It was exhilarating to be a part of the motley mobile club. Passing motorists stared at us as we drove from the factory through the winding roads that led to the Batemans' farm. Cars were still parked on the narrow road outside the Bateman home. We all parked a half-mile away and waited in our cars, killing time until the coast was clear.

"Do you really trust Jagger?" I asked Alexander. "Do you think now he really will keep the club for mortals?"

"I'm not sure. He's a sneaky guy. There is no telling what he'll do. Even with all the talks we've all had with him, he was *still* planning on making this a vampire club."

"What should we do?" I asked as several visiting cars from the farm headed home.

"I don't think we can let our guard down," he said. "I think we still have to watch his every move. And if you see or hear anything, let me know."

One by one the cars left the farm and eventually the Batemans' house lights went dark.

Scarlet and Onyx remained in the skull Beetle parked in a grassy hideaway, ready to honk if they spotted the lights switch back on.

I followed the vampire guys to the fence until Alexander stopped me.

"You stay here just in case. You can be our lookout."

I hated not to be in the middle of the action, but I knew that I was needed at my station. I climbed up the wooden fence, and from my vantage point I saw part of the crushed crops. I waited as Jagger, Sebastian, and Alexander headed through the field. Jagger attempted to erect bent stalks, but it was a useless mission.

"Something has to be done," I heard Alexander say.

"But what am I supposed to do?" Jagger huffed.

"Figure out something," Sebastian charged.

"We have to stop them before they come," Alexander said. "This has to be fixed, somehow."

Sebastian pulled out a few instruments he'd packed underneath his jacket.

"I have an idea," Alexander said.

In less than an hour they'd fixed the circle by making an "X" through it. This way it would be clear to any low-flying vampires that Dullsville wasn't a place for them to visit.

Alexander, Sebastian, and Jagger headed back toward me. I ran ahead to tell the others. I saw Luna in the front seat of the Mustang, chomping on gum and reading a magazine.

"They're finished," I said.

"Great," she said, leaning on the car door. "I can't stand any time away from my Sebastian."

I started off for Scarlet's Beetle when Luna stopped me.

"Do you mind doing me a huge favor?" She batted her eyelashes at me. She held out the magazine, her bony, pale arm in sharp contrast to the darkness. "Could you stick this in the back of the hearse for me?"

Normally I wouldn't want to do anything she asked of me. That was one favor I was willing to do. I was all about hearses.

I opened the back of the hearse and placed the magazine on the flatbed when I noticed something that wasn't a coffin—a long plank and more than a dozen feet of rope.

Jagger had made the crop circles and Luna wanted me to know it. It was clear she took pride in informing me that she and her brother were the nefarious type. Their game wasn't totally over. We'd still have to keep our eyes on him.

I was ready to blurt out my discovery when Alexander, Sebastian, and Jagger returned to their cars. For once they all appeared like three best friends just coming back from a night out on the town.

Not wanting to spoil their moment, I shut the hearse door.

As Sebastian gave Luna a kiss, I hugged Alexander extra hard. I was still skeptical of the Maxwells' future tricks, but for now I drew comfort in knowing I had the ultimate prize—Alexander.

12

Mortal Makeout

I shared my discovery with Alexander that evening, and we decided to keep the information between the two of us. We were both disappointed in Jagger, like we'd been with Sebastian. Both vampires seemed to let their own needs get in the way of what was best for others. I had wanted to see the good in Jagger and wasn't wholly convinced that he didn't have something else up his tattered sleeve. What it was, neither Alexander nor I knew. We just were aware that we had to be vigilant.

In the meantime I spent the following day at school doodling layouts for the Crypt. My imagination was wild with images of coffins, gravestones, and neon bats.

When I arrived home, my brother was yelping about some newsworthy event on the TV and dragged me into the family room.

"You have to see this," he said. "They struck again! Look."

"More crop circles?" I said, almost having heart failure. This time Junior Bateman was on TV.

"There it is, a big X. It wasn't there when we went to bed," the boy said.

"This time we had a video camera out," the father said.

Oh no, I thought. *We were going to be in trouble now.*

He showed the footage, fast-forwarded. "There isn't anyone on the video!" the boy cried, excited and horrified at the same time. "The aliens, they are invisible!"

"That is creepy," Billy Boy said. "I'm sure there is an explanation; I can't wait to meet Henry at Math Club and figure it out."

"There's only one explanation," I said truthfully. "Vampires."

My family shot me a quizzical look, and I rose and left for the mill.

I headed to the Crypt to wait for the vampires to rise. When I arrived, I saw a small truck parked outside. I didn't find anyone when I entered the main room. I was imagining myself dancing around on opening night when I heard hammering coming from downstairs. I tiptoed over to the Covenant door and turned the knob. It was locked. I pressed my ear to the door and I could hear more hammering. If the Covenant wasn't going to be used for a vampire club, what was it going to be used for?

I was wiping off the Crypt's bar when I heard the door unlock. I turned to look and a burly workman with a tool belt exited the Covenant and locked the door behind him.

He nodded and passed me by before I could say anything.

I dropped my towel on the bar and raced after him, but by the time I caught up with him he had already started his truck and was taking off down the gravel road.

When I returned, I was determined to get through the door. I stuck my boot against it and pulled, hoping the old lock might break, but it didn't budge. I had a bobby pin adorned with a skull stuck in my hair. I took it out and jimmied it into the lock. As much as I pried, the lock didn't come loose.

Scarlet found me fiddling with the knob.

"I didn't realize you guys were up," I said, shoving the pin in my pocket.

"Yes, some of us are still sleeping. We had a really wild night."

Onyx wandered out. "Good evening, Raven."

"Hey," I said. "I'm glad you both are awake."

When I realized no one else was following them, I returned my attention to the door. "What does this door lead to?" I asked her.

She shrugged her shoulders. "I don't know."

"No one will tell me," I said.

"Maybe it doesn't lead to anywhere," Onyx said.

"Then why is it locked?"

"To keep us from tripping down the stairs," Onyx said. "Duh."

I could only imagine what it led to. But maybe it was only the unfinished, never remodeled Covenant room. Maybe the worker was only reinforcing beams to make the main floor sturdier for dancing.

"I saw someone going in there once," Scarlet said. "Really late at night, when everyone else was done working. I saw Jagger go down there with one of the guys from the Coffin Club. When I spotted him and asked him what he was doing, he acted like I'd caught him doing something."

"So you think he's doing something sneaky?" Onyx said. "Why does everyone think he's such a bad guy?"

"Would you be so into him if he wasn't?" Scarlet teased.

I wasn't going to tell her that it was really Jagger who made the circles. She adored him so, and since he'd fixed the problem there was no reason to address it.

The mysterious locked door, on the other hand, was worth addressing.

"So what do you think it is?" I asked. "The underground club he said he wasn't going to have?"

"I have no idea," Scarlet said. "But I'd love to find out."

"We need a key," I said. "We can't break down this door. I know; I tried," I said with a smile.

"The only one with a key is Jagger," Scarlet said. "And I don't know how to get it from him."

We both turned to Onyx, who turned a paler shade of ghost white.

"I can't do it," she said. "He keeps his keys locked away. Besides, I don't want to do anything against him."

I was ready to continue putting pressure on her, but Scarlet let her off the hook.

"Do we know anyone else with a key?" Scarlet asked.

"That workman I just saw," I said. "But I don't know how to get it from him."

Then it hit me. Trevor. "Trevor wears a key around his neck and always shows it off to me like it's something I'd want."

"Do you think it goes to this door?" Scarlet asked.

"He and Jagger are friends, and apparently Trevor's dad was part of sealing the deal for the club," I said. "Trevor may not even have a clue what it goes to, but I think he holds the key to this door."

Scarlet's expression brightened. "I could always use an excuse to see him."

My stomach almost turned. My friend was excited about seeing the one person I loathed. But this time I'd be excited to see him, too.

Alexander and Sebastian were taking a break from the Crypt and hanging out at the Mansion. Normally I'd happily join them in their fun, not wanting to spend one nightly hour away from my true love, but curiosity was getting the best of me and, thankfully, of my new friend as well.

Scarlet picked me up in the Beetle. She cranked up the music and we sang at the top of our lungs until we got to the soccer field. We walked down the hill to the woods behind the field, recalling our music fest and laughing from the bottoms of our bellies. My cheeks hurt so bad I was afraid I'd split open my lip again. But what I didn't know was I already had.

"What's wrong?" I asked. Suddenly Scarlet was staring at my mouth.

"Oh no," I said.

Her eyes were a weird shade of red. Something had come over her. It was the scent and presence of blood. I backed away.

Scarlet took my arm. I was moments from a struggle. She was my friend and I knew she was fighting her internal impulse. I wasn't about to go down without a fight.

My mind raced. Instead of being turned by Alexander, I was going to be mauled by Scarlet. There was no one to defend me. She was a little bit bigger than me, and with her underworldly powers, I wasn't sure how I'd fare.

"You aren't going to attack me, are you?" I asked.

"No—why would you think so?" She did her best to close her eyes. She turned away from me and covered her face. "Could you please just fix it?"

I wiped my mouth with my sleeve and pressed a tissue to it.

Trevor was suddenly standing in the woods.

"What's going on in here?" he asked as I held the tissue to my lips. "I thought you'd at least wait for me!" he said.

"Don't be gross," I said.

Scarlet lit up in Trevor's presence.

"Why are you covering your mouth?" he asked me. "Grrr," he growled like a tiger. "Catfight? Don't stop on account of me."

"Cut it out," Scarlet said. "We were just in the neighborhood."

"In the high school's woods?" he asked suspiciously. "You shouldn't hang out here. Without me, of course."

"We wanted to see you," Scarlet said. "I wanted to see you."

She gave him a hug, her hands fiddling with his back pocket.

"What are you doing?" he asked.

Scarlet turned to me and held out her empty hand. Then she fiddled with the string around his neck. "What's this?"

"A necklace," he said.

She brought it out from his shirt. The key dangled below her hand.

"What's this key for?" she asked playfully.

"Nothing."

She pulled him tightly to her and planted a major kiss on his lips. As she did, his hands wrapped around her waist. She folded her arms around his neck and within a moment had unlaced the cord.

Trevor turned to me. He wiped his mouth with the back of his hand. Red lipstick was smeared across his skin.

For some reason I was resentful, but I didn't have time to think of that now. "We have to go," I said, pulling Scarlet away. She slipped the necklace into my hand.

"Jealous?" he asked. "Can't stand the sight of it?"

"Yes," I said. "I can't stand the sight."

I headed up the hill as Scarlet continued to say good night to my nemesis. Trevor's key hidden in my hand, I wondered what it led to and why it bothered me to see him kiss another girl.

* * *

It seemed like an eternity before Scarlet caught up with me by her car. Her hair was a little messy from her mortal make-out session.

"That was fun!" she said. "Let's do that again."

"Yeah . . . fun."

"He didn't even know I took his necklace."

We hopped into the car. The tunes were still blasting and she sang, but I was silent. She turned down the music.

"What's wrong?" she asked.

"Nothing." I was staring out the window, watching the trees as we passed them by.

"You seem weird. I shouldn't have been so PDA, sorry. I'm not into that, really. It was just that I had to get the key."

"I know."

"So what's up?"

"Nothing." I continued my zombielike staring.

"Do you . . . like Trevor?" she asked suddenly.

"No—are you crazy?" I was stunned by her accusation.

"Of course, you have a thing for him," she prodded.

"No, I don't!" I said with a laugh.

"I didn't know. You guys used to date?"

"No! Yuck! Are you kidding?"

"There's something between you two. I could feel it. Like a magnet."

"I'm in love with Alexander, if you haven't noticed."

"I didn't say you were going out with Trevor. I just thought you might have dated. There's that sexual tension between you two."

"I can't believe you just said that. He's such a creep! I

mean—not to offend you or anything, but me and him?"

"Opposites attract in a big way. Why do you think he likes me?"

"Because you are gorgeous and fun. What's not to like?" I asked.

"Thanks," she said sincerely. "But I'm not at all like those girls he normally goes after. Pink nails and luscious blonde hair. And now that I think of it . . . I'm like . . ."

"Yes?"

"You!"

"Me?"

"Duh! Why didn't I get it sooner!" Scarlet laughed.

"He likes you because of you," I said.

"But didn't he like Luna, too? Now this all makes sense."

"He likes girls. That's his thing. That's why I didn't want you to go out with him. He likes a lot of girls."

"No, with him it's more."

"Maybe he likes goths."

"Yes, because they remind him of you!"

"Stop!" I was close to covering my ears. I couldn't stand the thought. I was so in love with Alexander, nothing else mattered. No one else mattered.

"He's in love with you. Trevor Mitchell loves you," she teased.

"Please. Do you want me to be sick?"

"Sucks for me. I finally found a guy I'm crazy for and he only likes me back because he secretly wants to be with my friend."

"Enough, Scarlet. If you say any more, I'm going to jump out of this car!" I was only half-joking.

"So you don't mind if I continue to see him?"

"No, I don't," I said. "And guess what? If you want, I'll come to your wedding."

My blood was boiling by the time we got back to the factory. I was trying to shake off our conversation and also trying to figure out how we'd be able to see if this key was bogus or real without Jagger finding out.

"We need to have Onyx distract Jagger," I said when we got inside.

"Hopefully she can like I did with Trevor. But she's a lot shier than I am. So I'm not sure that is going to work."

"Hey, where were you guys?" Onyx asked.

"We went to see Trevor. Didn't you get my text?"

"Yes, but I was hanging out with Jagger." Onyx grinned.

"Speaking of Jagger. I need to ask a favor," Scarlet began.

"Sure, anything," Onyx said in a cheerful tone.

"We need you to keep Jagger occupied while we check out a few things here."

"You can't do that. This is his place. We are here to help, not snoop around."

"Not me," I said. "That's exactly why I'm here—to snoop around." I let out a laugh, but Onyx wasn't amused.

"If he finds out that I am tricking him, he won't want to see me anymore," she argued.

"You aren't tricking him. We're not going to steal

anything. Besides, we'll take all the blame," I said.

"Trust me." Scarlet put her hand on Onyx's shoulder. "He'll still want to see you. If I have my say."

Onyx paused for a moment.

"Please?" Scarlet asked. Now she was just as curious as I was.

"Okay," she said reluctantly. "But be quick. He's busy, and he doesn't like anything taking his time away from this club. Not even romance."

I pulled the string from around my neck and we raced to the door, monster boots slapping the Masonite floor.

I took a deep breath. I pushed the key in and it went in all the way. We both looked at each other and smiled.

Then I turned the key. And it clicked, unlatching the lock. We silently screamed in excitement. I turned the knob and opened the door.

"It worked. It worked!"

"What's going on?" a male voice said from behind us. We both jumped and screamed.

I pulled the key back out and slunk it into my pocket. Sebastian was back, along with Alexander.

"I missed you," Alexander said. "Where have you been?"

"With Trevor," Scarlet said proudly.

"Trevor?" he said. "That's the last time I leave you alone."

"This is the door I've been telling you about," I whispered to Alexander. "The key I have opens the door, and a workman was here building something down there. Jagger has been keeping this a secret. I have to get down there."

Just then Jagger and Onyx entered the main room.

"So do you like it here so far?" he asked.

"Yes, it looks great." I exclaimed with a smile as bright as his white hair.

"What about this?" Alexander said, pulling on the unlocked door handle and opening the door. "Where does it go to?" Alexander said, peeking in.

Jagger stepped in between and shut and locked the door. "Nothing now," he said.

Then Jagger turned on headbanging music and we all danced for a few hours. When we were all close to exhaustion, Jagger handed us some sodas from behind the bar.

"Now," he said. "I want everyone out. The Crypt is closed for the night."

"Where are we going to stay?" Scarlet asked.

"Here, but I have some things I need to finish—alone."

It made me wonder what he was doing that he wouldn't let us be involved in. And did it have to do with what was behind the locked door and down the stairs?

"Sure. I'll just get my things," I said. I'd put my backpack in the massive room filled with coffins when I arrived a few hours ago.

I had one chance to check the plans again. While Jagger tended to the last touches of the main dance floor, I tiptoed from the coffin room across the dank hallway into his office. The blueprints weren't lying out on his desk as they had been the last time.

I opened a metal filing case and in the drawer were the blueprints.

I unraveled them as quickly as I could and peeked at the ones marked "Covenant." I wanted to see what might have been if he had opened the vampire club.

I scanned it for any hidden clues. There was a rectangular box in the middle of the western wall. "Stage" was scrolled on it in pencil, and at the opposite end was another box marked "Covenant Altar."

Jagger was a master of cryptic design, and I knew that this underground club would be different but just as exciting as the Coffin Club's Dungeon.

Just like the coffins, tombstones, and skeleton decorations in the Crypt, Jagger intended to have a covenant altar for decoration in the Covenant. How awesome! I imagined dead vines around a cast-iron trestle. A coffin with goblets of juice on it to give the underground club the spice the torture chamber gave the Coffin Club. Spooky and cool at the same time.

The night we confronted Jagger about the crop circles, he had insisted the Crypt would be mortal only. But with that workman I spotted and the sounds of hammering that were coming from behind the locked door, I was still skeptical that the Covenant part of the club was going to remain closed on opening night.

Alexander and I had a midnight date at the cemetery. We hadn't seen each other alone in days and were both missing each other incredibly.

When I finally reached the back of the cemetery, Alexander hadn't arrived. Then I saw a figure lurking in the shadows. I raced to him, until I noticed blonde hair.

Trevor took my arm.

"It's okay," he said. "No one will notice."

"But I'm in love with Alexander," I told him firmly.

"And I'm in love with . . . you."

"You are not."

His stare was riveting. "But you know that I am."

He was right. I'd felt it for years.

Trevor stepped even closer to me. "Are you going to punish me for the rest of my life? Because I wear khakis and don't listen to that rancid music?" His green eyes bore through me to the bottom of my combat boots.

"I'm not punishing you. I don't love you. I love Alex—" I tried to step back, but he still held my arm.

Then he leaned in so close I thought our lips would touch. "But what if you hadn't met him?" he whispered. "And I came to you, like I did tonight. Just us. No one ever knowing."

I didn't turn away. "I don't know . . . I'd probably feel the same way I do now."

"But maybe you wouldn't," he urged in his sexy, almost breathless tone. "Are you really being true to yourself? We've known each other since we were kids. Not even Alexander can say that."

His fingers slid down my sleeve so they reached my hand. "We're not all that different. I've been saying that for years." He paused.

I was slightly afraid of what he'd do next.

His fingers slid down between mine. Trevor Mitchell was holding my hand. His grip was powerful, like that of a handsome athlete. He'd crossed a line. I was holding someone else's hand. This hand wasn't Alexander's, but it felt good, too. Like I was supposed to have held his hand and touched him. As if I'd been waiting all my life.

Trevor had grabbed me before but this was different. It didn't feel like he was trying to get back at me or put a notch on his headboard. It felt as if he was doing it because he wanted to more than anything else.

"It's okay," he said. He drew my hair back from my face. "This is about you and me now. Not anyone else. They can't keep us apart any longer. You can't keep us apart. This is meant to be." His movements were tender and his voice soft and sincere.

He pulled me to him so our chests were touching and he wrapped his arms around my waist. We stood face-to-face. He smiled his gorgeous smile.

No one was around. I wasn't scared. His hands were strong, and I felt a power from him. He smelled sweet, and his muscular body was warm. His eyes shined like the moonlight.

Before I could pull away, he leaned in and kissed me. His lips were magnetic and tender. I wasn't sure why I wasn't mad. For a moment, I was lost in his kiss.

I could feel his hands on my back pockets as he pulled me closer to him.

It took all my strength to turn away from him. For some reason I found his lips as riveting as his gaze.

"I can't," I said. "I came here for Alexander, not you."

"But you stayed for me." His tone was as sincere as his kiss.

It was then that he stepped back.

He held out the necklace he must have gotten from my pocket when he kissed me. The key swung back and forth like a medal.

"Monster Girl," he whispered.

"No—" I said. "No!!!"

I awoke with a jolt to find Nightmare pawing at my shirt.

I sat up. I could barely breathe. Nightmare jumped back, startled. Stunned, I reached out and grabbed my cat.

"It's just you pawing at me. Not that monster."

I cuddled my cat. Both our hearts were racing.

"I had a horrible nightmare, Nightmare. And not the good kind."

I got up, went to the bathroom and splashed water on my face, and tried to calm myself with a cup of water.

I switched the light on and hopped back into bed, put Nightmare on the pillow next to me, and pulled the covers over my head.

It was the first time I ever remember sleeping with the light on.

The following morning, when Becky and I were walking to our lockers, I couldn't hold it in any longer. "Do you ever have weird dreams?" I asked.

"All the time."

"Do they mean anything?"

"Some people say they do. But others don't. What did you dream?"

"That I . . . I can't even say it." I sunk my head.

"It was that bad?"

"Yes."

"Then I wouldn't worry about it. What did you eat before you went to bed?"

"I don't remember."

"It might have interfered with your sleep. That's all."

"I dreamed Trevor was in love with me." I spit it out like it was bad food.

"You've just now figured that out?" she asked.

"Why does everyone say that?"

"Because he's obsessed with you."

I shook off her comment. "But it gets worse, if you can imagine."

"Tell me."

"In the dream . . ."

"Yes?"

"I was in love with him, too."

She paused. "That's it?"

"I was in love with him. Don't you see why it was a nightmare?"

"It's just a dream, Raven. If dreams were real, then I'd be a ballerina."

"Really? I thought you'd say that I was secretly passionately in love with Trevor Mitchell."

"Gross! Besides, you are already in love with Alexander. There is no room for anyone else."

Relieved, I hugged Becky with the force of a million best friends. I was almost afraid I'd squash the life out of her.

Just before the sun set, I headed for the bathroom to get ready to go to the Crypt. Alexander's birthday was coming up and I still hadn't filled the vial. It wouldn't be too hard to prick my finger with a sterilized pin, but I'd been putting it off while being consumed with the Crypt. I was standing in front of the mirror, applying corpse white foundation, when I inadvertently broke the scab on the corner of my lip. The wound on my face reopened.

"Darn it!" I grumbled. I was so embarrassed by my crazy face. I reached for more cover-up as a little spot of blood arose. But then I remembered, I needed it this time.

I grabbed a Dixie Cup and let a few drops fall into it. I pushed my tongue against the inside of my cheek, forcing more blood to drip. I didn't need much to fill the small vial. Within a few minutes, I had enough. I washed my wound and pressed it with a wet tissue, holding it for a few minutes. It was then my mom opened the door.

I quickly stepped in front of the cup and stuck the vial in my pocket.

"What are you doing?" she asked.

"What are you doing?" I asked. "This is a private area."

"I didn't realize anyone was in here!"

"Well, I am! And I'm busy."

"I just needed your flat iron," she said. She opened the top drawer and grabbed the flat iron. I leaned over and pushed the cup behind a towel with my fingers, afraid that she'd notice the bloody cup in the mirror.

"What's that on your face?" she asked. "Tissue?"

"Mom, please."

"I can help you. That happens all the time. You just have to press it for a while and then use some cover-up. But don't pick at it."

"Mom, I know what to do." I leaned against the sink's counter, blocking the cup from her view, and tried to urge her out. "Please, just give me some private time."

"Well, if you need me, let me know," she said, closing the door behind her.

This time, I locked it.

I took the vial out of my pocket and carefully poured the Dixie Cup's contents into it. When I was finished, I crumpled the cup and threw it in the garbage can. I secured the vial and wrapped several tissues around it. I was exhausted, having come within seconds of being caught and having to explain to my mother why I was trying to fill a vial with blood. But ultimately I was pleased with my present for Alexander. I glanced at myself in the mirror. Dating a vampire wasn't as easy as I had always dreamed it would be.

Though the Crypt's opening was only a few days away, I turned my attention to Alexander's birthday. We had said we'd have a joint celebration at the Crypt, but I couldn't let this special day go by without a separate celebration. I'd spent the afternoon decorating the outside of the Mansion, and Jameson was kind enough to let me in to decorate Alexander's room with a few balloons. Now I was waiting impatiently in the gazebo for the sun to set. This was nothing new. My whole life, I was always waiting for the bright sun to disappear from view. But tonight I was ultra-impatient. It was my boyfriend's eighteenth birthday.

When the sun was out of view, I raced into the Mansion and up the grand staircase. I burst into Alexander's room and yelled, "Surprise!"

He stood, sleepy and dreamy. His hair was tousled and his shirtless chest was lean and pale against his dark boxer shorts.

Alexander crept out of his closet room into his regular attic room. He fought his way through a few dozen black balloons.

"I thought we were going to celebrate together," he said, "at the Crypt."

"We are. But not now. Get dressed."

"I mean both our birthdays. We were going to plan a joint party."

"I couldn't let yours go by without a private celebration." I gave him a big squeeze and an even bigger kiss, then anxiously danced around while he put on a T-shirt, jeans, and boots. Then I took him by the hand and led him to the Mansion's backyard.

I'd decorated the gazebo with black and purple streamers and bat, spider, and pumpkin balloons. Two floor-length candelabras lit the outdoor room.

"Wow—you went all out," he said. "But you always do."

"Happy eighteenth birthday, Alexander!" I said as he took in the decorations. "Wow—I'm dating a man."

"Weren't you always?"

"Yes, but there is something sexy about you being official. You are also two years older than me right now. I love an older man." I gave him a coy kiss.

"This is really cool how you decorated the backyard," he said. "You really are great at design."

"Thanks!" I said, beaming as bright as the moon. "Now I want to give you your gift."

"Isn't this party enough?"

"I don't think so." I handed him the small box.

He took his time unwrapping it.

"Hurry," I said.

"I'm trying to guess what it is."

"You're not supposed to guess. You are supposed to open it."

"Wow, Raven, this is really cool. He held it up to the candlelight. The snake is really awesome."

"There's something inside it."

He was surprised at first but shook it and noticed the movement of liquid.

"Me," I said.

He held the vial in his hands and pulled me toward him so intently. "Wow—I don't know what to say," Alexander murmured. "This is the best birthday ever," he raved.

He put the necklace on, and it looked amazing hanging around his neck.

"I'm never going to take it off," he said, giving me a juicy kiss.

Jameson arrived with a chocolate cake in the shape of a black palette with candles looking like small paintbrushes. As he and I began singing to Alexander, a third voice joined in.

Sebastian stepped out of the shadows as the song came to an end.

"Happy birthday, dude!" he said.

I couldn't help but invite one guest. I knew it would be romantic to have an intimate dinner with Alexander, but with his best friend in town, it wouldn't be the same if he wasn't included.

Jameson and Sebastian gave Alexander a large box with a bow. Inside was a guitar.

"Wow—thank you!"

"Now you can really have a garage band," Sebastian said.

The four of us sat at the table, eating cake and talking and laughing over the sound of a wailing guitar.

14

Rumor Mill

I was sleeping late as usual on the following weekend when I heard a knock on my bedroom door. I sat up to find Becky standing by my bed.

"What's going on?" I asked. "Am I late for school? It's Saturday, isn't it?"

But Becky wasn't interested in the days of the week. She handed me a cup of coffee from Javalicious.

"Thanks," I said.

"You'll need it. I just came from Matt's scrimmage."

"They played in the morning?"

"No—you slept most of the day away." She opened the curtains and I was blinded by the sun.

"No—" I said, squinting. I turned to look at my clock. It was four-fifteen.

"You need to be awake for this. Rumors are spreading that there are vampires living in Dullsville!" Becky said. "Can you believe that?"

"What?"

"I swear. Vampires, here in Dullsville. That's what people are saying."

"They said that when Alexander moved here. Trevor started that one, remember?"

"Well, they are saying it again."

"Where, when, and who?" I asked. "I need names."

"Well, you know it started when Sebastian bit Luna at Alexander's party."

"Yes, but they don't have proof that really happened." I yawned.

"But it's more than that. The soccer snobs and other students were weirded out when Alexander, Sebastian, Scarlet, Onyx, Jagger, and Luna came to the game," Becky confessed.

"That's not news. . . ."

"They said they're . . . freaks."

"They've said that about me all my life. That's nothing new either."

"You know how people talk. Jagger and his entourage don't go to school and are only seen at night. Scarlet drives a skull and Jagger a hearse."

"Yes, I guess it does look a bit weird to Dullsvillians. But totally normal to me." I smiled with pride.

"Matt said Trevor told him that Scarlet has fangs, and others are saying they live in graves in the factory."

Coffins, I wanted to correct her.

"Trevor will say anything," I said. "And they live in the

mill because they are making it into a dance club."

"I know that, and you know that. But it's not just Trevor. Even Matt thinks things are strange."

"He does?"

"But not too strange. He knows Alexander. But like me, he's a bit worried that those guys are living in that creepy factory."

"They are fine. Really."

"But there's more."

"Yes?"

"No one wants to go to the club now."

"Are you serious?"

She nodded.

"He's going to be opening up the Crypt in just two days! If no one comes, then he's going to close it." Now I was the one freaking out.

"I'm sorry to be the one to tell you," she said sincerely.

"No, I'm glad you did. I'd hate for that part to be a surprise."

I had to get to the factory. Jagger couldn't close the Crypt before he opened it.

As soon as it was dark, I rushed to the Sinclair Mill and whisked past Scarlet and Onyx without even saying hi and headed straight for Jagger, Alexander, and Sebastian, who were having celebratory drinks.

"What's wrong?" Alexander said.

"Everyone at school is saying that vampires are living here. Now no one wants to come to the club's opening. We have to do something. We only have two days!"

"What do you mean?" Jagger said.

"Just that. Rumors about us—you guys. That you are vampires. Sebastian bit Luna. You don't go to school and are never seen in the daylight. These people live for that stuff. Then you throw in a skull car and a hearse. I told you it wasn't safe for you to have an underground club here. Now do you see what I mean?"

"How are we going to open if no one shows?" Sebastian wondered.

Failure wasn't in Jagger's vocabulary. "They'll have to show," he said defiantly.

"Dude, we have to have girls here to make this work," Sebastian said. Luna shot him a dirty look. "And guys, too."

"Stop. Let me think," Jagger said. "What if we change? We'll have to make our look be more 'friendly.'"

"So you guys are going to be preps?" I asked.

"It's a thought."

"Your hair is white with blood-red tips," I said.

"I can dye it brown."

"And Luna—her pink hair?"

"I'm not touching my hair," she said.

"And what about all your tats? You're just going to scrape them off?"

"We'll cover ours up," Jagger said. He didn't like that I was challenging his idea.

"No. You can't change who you are. I've been this way my whole life and I've never changed," I said firmly.

"And they accepted you?" Jagger charged.

They all turned to me, already knowing the answer.

"This is about business," Jagger said. "Not about making friends."

"But it is," I said. "You can't not be who you are. That's why I love you guys. If you change, then you'll be like everyone else in town. I can't have you do that. There's got to be another way."

"Then can you tell me what it is?" Jagger challenged. "I have already invested a lot of money in this. You told me how everyone in town would come here to dance. Now you are telling me they aren't. What do you suggest I do?"

There was only one person in Dullsville who could change everyone's mind.

"Trevor Mitchell," I said. "If he's on board, then everyone in town will be, too."

"We'll have to do more than just show up to his soccer game," Jagger said. "This time, we'll have to make him a partner."

It wasn't too long before Scarlet returned with Trevor. Apparently all it took was a few texts, several lip-locks, and the promise of even more power in Dullsville than he already had to convince him to accept a one-on-one meeting with Jagger.

Jagger didn't hold the meeting in his office. With its walls adorned with cemetery sketches and a tarantula creeping in an aquarium, not to mention its location across the hall from the room filled with coffins, it wasn't the ideal setting. Instead Jagger held the meeting with the blonde jock in a small, vacant room on the top floor.

I paced outside the room while Sebastian and Alexander downed blood-filled glasses and the girls calmed their nerves by painting their nails black.

There wasn't a clock in the Crypt, but it seemed like the two were holed up for ages. Finally I couldn't bear it anymore.

"More cobwebs are going to form if they don't hurry," I said to the gang. "What are they talking about in there?"

Just then the door creaked open. Trevor didn't make eye contact but just headed down the stairs.

We all had our hearts in our stomachs, waiting for the result.

"He agreed!" Jagger declared proudly. "We're back in business."

"Yay!" Scarlet, Onyx, and I cheered.

Scarlet raced downstairs after Trevor to take him home.

"It means your portion goes down," Jagger said, putting his arm around Sebastian. "We all had to give a little." Jagger opened a Romanian wine bottle and poured thick red liquid into tiny shot glasses. Everyone but me took one. I held one filled with cranberry juice.

"Here's to the Crypt," Jagger said. "And sacrifice."

Dullsville High had an unusual air about it. Instead of the normal school malaise or enthusiasm about sports and upcoming dances, this Monday the halls were filled with a different kind of buzzing, and the excitement couldn't be contained in the whispers. A crowd had gathered at the end of the hallway by the gym. Becky and I pushed our way through, dying to find out what all the fuss was about. Dance music was being played.

"It's awesome," Trevor said, handing out flyers. "Nothing in town like it."

"This will be cool," one student said. "I'll tell my friends."

"I can't wait until it opens."

Nothing was cool in town without Trevor's stamp of approval. Even a few teachers were more interested in the club than they were in shutting down Trevor's makeshift promotional stand.

"I'm all out, people, but I'll have more tomorrow," Trevor said.

Students dispersed with their plastic vampire teeth, stickers, and flyers.

My nemesis spotted me and his smile grew even bigger.

"So now I'm part owner of a club," he said to me. "I'll definitely have all access. I might even be able to remove your name from the VIP guest list if you're not too careful."

"I don't think that will happen. You aren't that powerful."

He got up in my face. "I'm not sure you know all the terms of our agreement," he said, his green eyes blazing through me.

"What does that mean?" I said, squaring off against him.

"The terms and conditions of me becoming part owner of said club, the Crypt. But that's not important now, because I also heard it's not too much longer till your birthday. Then you'll get the surprise you've been waiting for all your life."

"Your funeral?"

He laughed.

It was hard for me to make direct eye contact with Trevor after I had had that lust-filled dream about him. I felt that somehow he knew I'd dreamed it—like it showed in my face.

As he packed up his iPod, he said, "I'm missing something, and I think that you might know where it is."

"Geez, your brain? Intelligence? A sense of goodwill toward man? We could be here all day."

"A certain necklace with a key. I thought you might know where it is."

"Hey—if you need to keep your house key around your neck, then you have bigger worries. Try pinning it to your mittens next time."

"It's not a big deal, really. Jagger can just make me another. Besides, it might have slipped off when I was making out with Scarlet in the woods."

"I'm sure that's what happened."

He grasped my wrist. "Don't worry, Monster Girl, you'll get your chance when we have that one dance on opening night. Jagger promised me many things. And that was one."

"Jagger can't promise you anything about me!" I said, withdrawing my arm. "I'm not for sale!"

"Fine, then I'll just stop telling people about the club.

And tell them about the ghouls who live in the Sinclair Mill instead."

"You said you'd help!" I said, getting in his face.

"For a small dance . . . ," he retorted, his gaze softening.

I imagined the Crypt's opening night. The vampires and me standing around, with rooms empty of clubsters. Jagger, Scarlet, and Sebastian tearing down the decorations, packing up their coffins, and driving the hearse, skull Beetle, and Mustang back to Hipsterville.

"Fine, you'll have your stupid dance," I said through gritted teeth. "Just keep posting and handing out those flyers."

I turned away and stormed off.

"I knew you'd come around to my way of thinking," he called after me. "You'll be begging for more."

Just after sunset, I stormed over to the Sinclair Mill. Jagger was at the bar on his cell while the rest of the gang was hanging out.

"How could you?" I shouted.

"What's wrong?" Alexander asked.

"He knows what's wrong!" I said, pointing to Jagger.

"Me?" Jagger said naively.

"How could he what?" Alexander said with great concern.

"Sell me off to Trevor!" I was so upset my fists were balled up and my lips were quivering.

"It's one dance," Jagger said.

"I'm not for sale!" I said.

"What did you do, Jagger?" Alexander's pale face flushed red with anger.

"Dude, what were you thinking?" Sebastian said.

"That's all he asked for. I tried money, but he said he wanted one dance with Raven on opening night. I figured you wouldn't care. It's just one dance."

"Are you kidding? You've crossed the line!" Alexander rose. "Raven is not for sale." He was face-to-face with Jagger. Alexander was madder than I was.

"I figured Raven wouldn't care. It was for the good of the club, and she was so happy to have it open," Jagger said. "But fine. I'll call him and tell him the deal's off." He picked up his cell phone.

"Stop—" I said. "Don't call him."

"Are you crazy?" Alexander exclaimed.

"It's just one stupid dance. And it can be a fast dance. And you'll be right next to me," I told Alexander.

"I'll be there, too," Sebastian said, to the chagrin of Luna.

"And so will I," Jagger added firmly.

I was truly touched with my vampire bodyguard entourage.

"This sounds exciting now." I beamed.

Scarlet was sulking. It should have been her Trevor was asking to dance with.

"It's just to get back at me," I said, putting my arm around her. "It's all that boy lives for."

15

Birthday Bash

A year ago today, my mom presented me with two home-made cakes, one in the shape of a one and the other in the shape of a six; Becky gave me a pewter necklace with a tiny charm of a bat; and I heard the news of a family moving into the Mansion on Benson Hill.

The year that followed was a dream come true. Not only did I feel one year older, I felt many years wiser. I'd met and fallen in love with a vampire. I'd been shown the Underworld, his family, his friend, his nemesis, and experienced love on a level that was truly out of this world. It only made me excited for what this next year might bring me.

But most exciting was that the Crypt would be opening tonight.

I came downstairs to the sound of "Happy Birthday" being sung at different octaves by my family.

Sweet sixteen had been received with more fanfare

than not-so-sweet seventeen. But even so, my family didn't let my birthday go unnoticed.

My dad kissed me on the cheek. My mom gave me a huge squeeze and handed me a card.

I quickly opened it to find a birthday check.

My brother slid a card to me across the table where he was eating breakfast. Enclosed was a gift card to our local coffee shop.

"Thanks, Billy. This is an awesome gift! Really."

I gave my little brother a hug. He was surprised by my sudden display of affection and barely hugged me back.

"And tonight we're going to celebrate!" my mom said. "I got reservations at Pip's."

Pip's was a mom-and-pop restaurant that specialized in one-of-a-kind meals, cheesy decor, and making a big deal about birthdays.

"Pip's? I'm seventeen, not four," I said. "Besides, tonight I was going to go out with my friends."

My mother sighed. "But I made reservations."

The club was opening, and I was supposed to sit in a restaurant while all of Dullsville High was going to be bopping to the music of the Skeletons?

"Well, it's your birthday. If you don't want to celebrate it with your family . . . ," my mom said, deflated.

"Of course I do." I tried to hide my apathy.

"I invited Becky and Matt, too."

"I appreciate it," I said.

My family quickly dispersed, engrossed in upcoming meetings, work, and school. It wasn't long before my little celebration was over and I found myself alone.

When I reached the front door, there was a bouquet of flowers with a note.

Happy Birthday.
Love,
Alexander

I didn't have time to put them in a vase. Instead, I took them with me and hopped in Becky's truck.

"Those are beautiful," she said.

"He's so sweet," I said. "He remembered."

"Haven't you been talking about your birthday all the time?" she asked.

"Pretty much," I said. We both broke into giggles.

Becky handed me a long box.

"Thanks," I said, ripping it open. It was a black shirt with THE CRYPT written in white skeleton bone letters.

"This is the best present ever! How did you get it?"

"I have connections," she said proudly.

When I opened my locker I expected something nefarious to jump out. Instead, a bat-shaped box of chocolates was waiting for me.

"Aww," I said. "Look what Alexander gave me."

"Those look delish!" Becky said, almost salivating. "If you need someone to share those with, you've got your girl."

I put the chocolates in my bag, wanting Alexander's

presence to be close to me. I didn't have the protection of the darkness. The sun was out, and so was the blonde-haired monster. I didn't know what my nemesis had planned, so I was on edge the entire day.

By the time I got home, I was fatigued. I plopped down on my bed and opened my backpack to get out the chocolates when I found something shiny.

It was a small present with white wrapping paper and a silver bow.

I opened the card to see what Alexander had snuck in my bag. The tiny card read, "Happy Birthday, Monster Girl."

I pushed it aside. No telling what was inside. I hung out in my room, texting Becky, checking messages, and putting laundry away. But nothing could get my mind off the shiny box. Finally curiosity got the best of me.

I slowly opened the box. I knew it was going to be something dead.

It was worse. Far worse than opening the present to find an empty box. What I saw was by far more nefarious and cunning. Trevor really got me this time.

I found a small bracelet with RAVEN engraved in sterling silver, with two black leather bands united at a silver clasp. It was beautiful.

Warmth flooded my veins, and my heart was reluctantly but still deeply moved. I was touched. And he knew I would be. Trevor took the time to buy something real for me. Instead of giving me a gag gift, he gave me the kind of present one gives to a best friend or true love. And it made me wonder if this was a sign of his feelings for me, especially after that powerful dream. For some reason I couldn't wipe the smile off my face.

Trevor Mitchell wanted to wrap himself around my wrist.

I put the bracelet back in the box and began to close it when, at the last second, I opened it again. No one was watching. I had to see what the bracelet looked like on. I placed it on my wrist and closed the clasp. The letters shined and the leather straps were really cool. Trevor did have good taste. I imagined the girlfriend he'd ultimately have, him bathing her in jewels and then going out with someone else.

Trevor knew I couldn't return it. First of all, it would have been rude—even for me. Who else could wear this gift with my unusual name on it? He wouldn't be able to get his money back on a custom design.

And if I wore it to school, Trevor would know I liked it, and he'd never wipe the gloating smile from his face.

And worse, if I showed it to Alexander, my boyfriend would be really ticked off. Trevor ultimately had won his game.

No one would know if I wore it for a while. I imagined that he'd taken the time to have it ordered, bought it, and boxed it up, all while thinking of me. It was odd, to say the least. And odder still that I didn't want to remove it quite yet.

But then I got a text from Alexander. He must have woken up early, before the sun set, and was restless in his coffin. And then I remembered how real boyfriends behaved. The kind that didn't kiss one girl and give presents to another. I quickly unclasped the bracelet and buried it, along with any pleasant thoughts of Trevor, in my dresser drawer.

Alexander, handsome in a classy suit coat and black jeans, arrived at our front door with a bouquet of flowers.

"But you already gave me flowers this morning," I said.

"I couldn't be there to see your face," he said, handing them to me. "Now I can."

I gave him a huge kiss and we stepped inside.

"Those are beautiful," my mother said, coming down the stairs and wrangling an earring in her ear. "I'll get a vase."

"I'd like to take one to dinner," I said.

"You can wear it in your hair," my mother said like a former hippie.

The last time I'd wanted flowers pinned on me was when Alexander gave me a corsage for the Snow Ball. I'd pricked my finger and he had made a strange expression I'd since come to find out was that of a vampire looking at fresh blood. I made sure not to tempt my boyfriend in front of my parents.

Instead of using pins and needles, Alexander was kind enough to clip the flower in my barrette.

When we got to the restaurant, it was hard not to think of the Crypt, even while so much fussing was going on. I was so anxious to get to the club. Even though we could sit down immediately, we'd be ordering appetizers, main courses, and desserts. It would be ages until we'd be able to meet the gang at the dance club.

Alexander must have sensed my anxiousness. He rested his hand on my twitching leg.

I was suddenly overcome with a sense of peace. I was relaxed. I scanned the table. I had a great mother and father, and though they never understood me, they still were always there for me. My brother, Billy, who was the biggest pest in the world, was texting Henry as if no one knew and would occasionally answer a question without even looking up. But still, there he sat, celebrating my birthday. My best friend, who was there for me, laughing and gossiping since the day we met, and her boyfriend. And of course, the love of my life, my vampire soulmate, who had taken my blood as his own. I realized I was with the most gorgeous guy— holding his hand and wearing one of the flowers he'd given me in my hair. I didn't want to be anywhere else.

And when that horrible moment came, when the wait-staff brought a candlelit dessert and my family and a few patrons sang "Happy Birthday," and I blushed beet red, I kind of liked it.

I looked around the room as the single candle blazed in the sundae. I had a best friend, a family, and my true love. What else could I want?

I really had everything I wanted sitting at the table— except the one thing I'd been wishing for since I was in kindergarten: to become a vampire. I closed my eyes, wished, and blew out the candle to cheers and applause.

I wondered just how many more years I'd be making that wish.

As we got out of the Mercedes and headed through the back alley to the Crypt, Alexander pulled me aside.

"This is my real gift. I didn't want to freak out your parents."

"Then what were the flowers?"

"Just a prelude gift."

"What is it?" I asked coyly.

"You'll see."

He handed me a box. I only hoped it wasn't a bracelet that said "Raven." I wouldn't know what to do.

I opened the box. There wasn't a bracelet. Instead there was a slender silver eternity ring with petite black diamonds. The center diamond was in the shape of a small heart.

Chills ran down my spine. I almost fainted right there in the alley of the Crypt.

"Alexander—I don't know what to say. This is beautiful!"

"This way you'll always know that just because I haven't turned you doesn't mean we can't be together forever."

"How can you afford this?" I asked.

"How could I not afford it?"

"I've never had anything real—besides a pearl necklace my parents gave me last year for my birthday."

"Just put it on."

Tears welled in my eyes. Nothing I'd ever owned twinkled liked the ring I was now holding. I slid it on my right ring finger.

"It fits?" he asked eagerly.

"It's like having the stars on my finger," I said, jumping up and down.

I reached up to him and gave him the most passionate kiss I'd ever given.

"Get a room, dudes. Or at least a car," Sebastian said, slapping Alexander on the back.

I showed Sebastian the ring.

"Are you getting married?" he asked. "Dude—"

"It's not an engagement ring," I said. "It's an eternity ring."

Luna spied the glistening ring and bore her fangs at me. The expression she wore spoke volumes.

"It's time we get to the club. We've been waiting forever for it to open!" Alexander said.

When I turned down the alley to the mill, I saw an image even I couldn't have ever envisioned in Dullsville. A long line snaked around the corner of the factory and led up to the Crypt. Every student in Dullsville High was standing, texting, and gossiping in line, waiting for a chance, like me, to dance in a club. I was lucky to be in Sebastian's and Luna's company so we could walk past the sea of would-be clubsters and make our way to the entrance.

A sign in blood-red letters marked the entrance: CHECK ALL CELL PHONES, CAMERAS, AND MP3 PLAYERS. PHOTOGRAPHS PROHIBITED. A bouncer was checking all electronic devices.

When we entered, Sebastian and Luna disappeared into the Crypt while I stood spellbound. Alexander stood behind me, his hands on my shoulders. A lot had changed since I'd last been to the factory. The scene was truly magical.

Dullsville finally had a place, besides the Mansion, where I truly belonged.

Gray arched columns made the once-flat ceiling appear curved. Lightning flashed against the windows, and thunder rumbled over the music as if there were a nasty storm outside the club. The center stage was magnificent. It was in the shape of a large coffin. Headstone doorways had handles resembling skeleton bones. Votives and LED torch lighting hung on the walls like a creepy tomb. The bar, too, was shaped like a giant coffin. Bottles covered in fake cobwebs were on wooden racks. The dance area was illuminated by candelabra chandeliers flickering LED lights. Two metal cages with twisted wrought iron were in the corners for dancing clubsters. Neon exit signs hung above all outgoing doors. An open coffin rested next to an erect one with signs inviting customers to step inside. For a small price, a photographer dressed as a caretaker took pictures.

The conservative students raved about the new club. Any club party with loud music was the chance to let loose and be away from nagging parents.

"Wow!" I said. "This is what I've always dreamed of."

I found Scarlet and Onyx already dancing.

While Alexander and Sebastian tried to find Jagger, I jumped onto the dance floor and rocked with my vampire friends.

I noticed Luna, off in the corner, waiting for Sebastian to return. She was a misfit, even in her brother's club. Aloof and unfettered, she just observed the goings-on around her. Scarlet and I ran over to her and dragged her onto the dance floor with us. It was as if she was relieved, finally having some friends of her own to hang out with. It wasn't long before her pink hair was tossing back and forth as we all danced to the morbid music.

Exhausted, I took a break. It was then I caught sight of the curious door—only tonight it was adorned like a grave marker and had a skeleton-bone handle.

"Do you know where Jagger is?" I asked Scarlet when we headed off to the bar. "I want to try that door again and I don't want him to see me."

"What?" She tried to shout over the music.

"That tombstone door. We still don't know what it leads to. This could all be a ruse for something nefarious underground."

"You can check it out," she said, uninterested. "I want to dance. I think I see Trevor." She slipped into the crowd while Luna and Onyx continued to dance.

I made my way through wall-to-wall clubsters until I reached the grave marker door. There was so much going on, I was sure no one would notice me trying to sneak in.

I had put the key in and turned the lock when someone grabbed my hand.

"Time to dance," Trevor said.

Before I could shake free I was back on the dance floor, staring at Trevor Mitchell.

Where were Alexander, Sebastian, and Jagger to protect me?

I stood motionless, with my arms folded.

"You can move better than that," he said.

He put his hands on my waist and shook my hips back and forth.

"Get off!" I said.

"The dance doesn't start until you do!" he said.

Then I thought, *What difference does it make?* I was as close to Trevor as I was to anyone else on the dance floor.

I let the song take over me and I danced my heart out. All at once I was lost, dancing with Trevor. His green eyes burned through me as if we were the only two on the dance floor. He put his hand around my waist and drew me to him, so close our bodies touched. I could feel his rock-hard stomach against mine. He stared at me intently and a smile crept across his face. I was in his clutches. I knew any moment Trevor was going to kiss me.

Suddenly Alexander was standing next to Trevor. There was no denying Alexander was ready to take him off the dance floor—physically.

"It's okay," I said. I pulled Alexander close. "That dance is over now. The rest are saved for you."

Trevor watched me as I snuggled with Alexander. I checked back and Trevor was dancing with a group of girls, as if I didn't exist anymore.

The following morning I stumbled into the kitchen to grab a cup of coffee.

My mom caught sight of my ring.

"That's gorgeous. Where did you get it?"

"Alexander gave it to me."

"Sweetheart—that's real."

"I know. Can you believe this? I don't deserve something this beautiful."

"Maybe you're too young to get a gift like that," she said with a crinkle in her brow.

"I just turned seventeen! And Alexander's eighteen. Too young?"

"I didn't mean it like that."

"I'm sorry I snapped."

"Did he ask you anything when he gave it to you?"

"Like getting down on one knee?" I asked, slightly horrified at her overreaction to my good news. "No, he didn't. Why does everyone have to take this as more than it is?"

If she was this freaked out about a ring, I couldn't imagine what she'd say if I told her I wanted to turn into a vampire—for real.

"Maybe we should talk," my mom said.

"About the birds and bees? I think we've been over that."

"No, about your future. College. Getting out of town. Alexander."

"What, now you don't approve of him?"

"Of course I do. I think he's been amazing for you. I just hope you'll go to college."

"You met dad at college. It's not my fault that I met my true love in high school. Besides, can't I just enjoy my birthday present?"

"I just want you to make sure you are as focused on school as much as you are on relationships."

"Well, you know I have never been focused on school." We both had a small chuckle. "If Alexander decides to study in Romania, I'm up for it," I assured her.

"It shouldn't be about what Alexander wants. That's what I'm trying to talk to you about."

"Have I ever done anything in my life I didn't want to do?" I asked candidly.

"Uh . . . no. I wish you had—it would have made my life a lot easier."

"Have I ever succumbed to peer pressure?" I asked.

"No. You are the antithesis of that."

"Then why can't you trust me?"

"Because I know what love does. It makes you think things—that the world is more romantic than it is."

"Is that so bad? You have Dad, this house, and Billy and me."

"You are right, but—"

"I've been pretty miserable most of my life. For almost a year now, I've really enjoyed this town. I have a great boyfriend and I've met a lot of people that I connect with. I haven't gotten into trouble and my grades have been pretty good."

"I was always hoping you'd be able to graduate and find a passion beyond . . ."

"Vampires?"

"Yes."

"I'll go to college, Mom. I want to be an editor for a fashion mag. You think Alexander would go out with me if I were just a slacker? He has standards, too."

"I know. Alexander is an amazing guy."

"I want to show you something," I said. She followed

me to my bedroom and I took out the bracelet buried in my drawer from Trevor.

"This could be my future," I said.

"Where did you get this?"

"Trevor Mitchell."

"Trevor? That is unexpected."

"I know . . . so when you worry about my future, you can think about this one, too," I said. "We could be having the same conversation about a different person. And do you know what it would be? A future with a gorgeous guy who thinks about himself more than anyone else. And guess what? While I'm watching him pursue his soccer dream, he'd be sneaking off with a leggy blonde cheerleader."

My mom sat on my bed, handling the bracelet. "I knew I'd found Mr. Right when I met your father. My mother wanted me to wait, too, and date different guys in college. And if I had, I wouldn't have been happy. I wouldn't have been in love. And I wouldn't have had you."

I heard my dad coming up the stairs.

"Paul," she called to him. "Look what Alexander gave Raven." My mom proudly held out my hand to him.

"Moving a little fast, aren't we?" he asked. "Shouldn't Alexander be talking to me first—or should I be talking to him?"

"No one needs to talk to anyone," she said, softening the blow. "It was a special present Alexander gave Raven. And I think we should be happy for her and leave it at that."

My dad examined the ring. "Wow—is that real?"

I nodded.

"The boy has good taste. Although I already knew that," he said with a wink.

That evening I met Alexander just after sunset at the Mansion. With only a day until the joint birthday party at the Crypt, I didn't want anything to get in the way of it—including unwanted vampires. I was dressed and ready to go to the club, but when I met Alexander in his room, he wasn't ready. He was rummaging around in his closet.

Alexander had other plans.

"Phoenix needs to come to the Crypt tonight," he said. "I'll have Jameson drop you off at the club."

"Tonight?" I asked, goose bumps shuddering down my spine. The thought of seeing Phoenix again—especially when I knew he was really Alexander—thrilled me. And his being on a secret mission made him that much sexier to me.

"Nothing major happened last night—no unknown vampires popping in—or at least none that we knew about," he said. "But it's not like the Maxwells to cave so easily. The Covenant door still remaining locked means Jagger is planning to use it for something. We can't wait any longer."

"I agree," I said.

The more I fell in love with the Crypt, the harder it would be for me to lose it if unknown vampires started coming.

"We have to have proof that vampires aren't being

invited," I said, "and Phoenix has the power to do that."

I watched as Alexander continued to scour through his closet.

"Phoenix can save this club, too," I said. "If it wasn't for him taking over the Coffin Club and, at the last moment, giving the reigns over to the clubsters, Jagger wouldn't even have that club. He's almost like a super-hero."

"All right," Alexander said, pulling out a pair of black leather pants and a motorcycle jacket and tossing them on the bed. "It's time for you to go. I'll see you at the club."

Glaring at his sexy outfit strewn on his coffin, I almost had a change of heart. "This isn't easy, you know. I'd rather be with you—as Alexander, Phoenix, or whomever—than alone in that nightclub."

"Get out of here," he said playfully as he put on a tight white T-shirt.

I did my best to tear myself away from my handsome boyfriend.

"And don't forget that British accent," I called back to him as I left his room. "It goes right through my heart!"

17

Familiar Visitor

Jameson kindly drove me to the Sinclair Mill–turned-fabulously-macabre dance club. It seemed to take forever as the Creepy Man drove at a zombie's pace. After I finally arrived I was hanging outside the Crypt with Scarlet when I heard the sound of a motorcycle pull up to the factory.

"Maybe it's the police," I heard one clubster say.

A purple-haired biker raced through the alley and parked his Harley.

"I think that's Phoenix!" Scarlet said. "What's he doing here?"

"I don't know," I said.

"This club isn't supposed to be open to outside vampires," she said as if taking offense to her special VIV—Very Important Vampire—status. She stormed after him, and I followed close behind, but by the time we reached the entrance he was already going inside.

"Line cutter!" I heard a few clubsters shout.

"My best friend dates the owner!" Scarlet shouted back.

Scarlet grabbed my arm and we quickly ducked inside so as not to make any more enemies than I normally had.

I spotted a handsome guy with purple hair talking to Jagger by the dancing cages.

We pushed through the crowd of dancers and snuck up behind them, eavesdropping on their conversation.

"I saw the crop circle," Phoenix said. "So I came to check out your place."

"Uh . . . we got rid of that. The plans for the club have changed," Jagger said.

"This place looks cool!" Phoenix continued. "What are you serving?"

"I really must tell you—"

"This club might be better than the Coffin Club," Phoenix said, slapping Jagger on the back.

"You think so?" Jagger was overcome with the attention. He beamed like a star. "Romeo—get this man a Lethal Injection. It's the house special," he said. "So, how did you hear about us?"

"Like I said before, a crop circle. I figured you were starting a new vampire club. But this town isn't known for vampires. So I thought I'd come and check it out."

"Well, there are a few here among us. But that's what I need to tell you about. I made a deal with my buddies," Jagger said. "This club will be slightly different from the Coffin Club."

"What do you mean by 'different'?"

It was as if Jagger was afraid to admit that the club would be mortals only. "You think this should be like the Coffin Club, with a Dungeon, too? My friends persuaded me . . . I was a fool to listen. You have to see what I have here. Let me give you a tour."

I followed behind so as not to be too conspicuous. When they passed the Covenant room door, Phoenix stopped.

"What's this?" Phoenix asked. "Another club?"

"That's not just another club—it is *the* club. The Covenant," he said proudly. "More private than the Dungeon."

Phoenix's eyes lit up. "So this is where the vampires are?"

"Yes. They'll be here."

"So you have planned another vampire club? Something you can't share with your 'buddies' but you can with me, your old friend?"

"It's only for special members."

"Vampires? Does anyone else know?" he pressed.

"No, it's a secret. No one knows. I was waiting for a special occasion to open it."

"Ah . . . the element of surprise," Phoenix said.

"Exactly," Jagger said.

Phoenix scanned the crowd of mostly mortal dancers and put his hand on Jagger's shoulder. "Some surprises are best left undone."

"I'm not sure what you mean," Jagger said, confused.

"Look around here, Jagger," Phoenix said. "This town,

this club. It's full of mortals. No vampires live here. You could put us all in danger by inviting indiscreet vampires here," he charged.

"Well, a few vampires and their friends do live here."

"It's not safe for you to run a vampire club in a town this small."

"And it's not safe for you to come to my club and tell me how to run it."

"You know what happened between us at the Coffin Club. It can happen here, too," Phoenix pressured.

Jagger was really heated. His face flushed red like the fiery dyed tips of his white hair.

"You don't know the truth. That club isn't meant for you. Maybe in the beginning I thought it would be cool to have a second Coffin Club. But you know, I think this one will be unique, too. It's meant as a special club for my friends to celebrate their birthdays in. A surprise. One they'll never forget. You've come all this way, and you were lucky I let you in. But this club and the one below are for mortals only," Jagger said, "unless you are one of my closest vampire friends, which I'm sorry to say you are not."

Jagger waited, poised for a fight. But when Phoenix smiled, Jagger's body relaxed.

I couldn't believe it. I'd done so much sneaking in and asking questions, but it had taken only seconds for Phoenix to get more answers than I had in a month.

"Then I guess my work is done here," Phoenix said like a cowboy in a Western movie.

But Jagger continued to soften. It was unlike him to

send someone out of his club with a bad taste in their mouth.

"Second round is on the club as well," Jagger said. "It was good of you to come this far to check us out. Tell your mortal friends about it. And if I do ever open it to vampires, you'll be the first to know."

Phoenix made his way back to the bar, sipping his Lethal Injection. I wanted to go and hang out with my boyfriend's alter ego, but I knew I would look like I was flirting with someone other than Alexander. Several girls sidled up to him and batted their eyelashes at him, doing their best impression of femmes fatales. It took all my strength not to clobber them. I couldn't tell Scarlet who he really was, so instead we hung by the bar sipping sodas and discussing Phoenix and Jagger's encounter.

"What kind of surprise do you think Jagger has planned down there?"

"Maybe a big birthday cake."

"I love cake," Scarlet said. "Or maybe he'll turn you into a vampire."

"I think that's Alexander's job."

Just then Phoenix turned around. Hearing the name Alexander was natural to him.

I winked at him, and suddenly Luna was standing before him.

"My brother told me about you," she said. "Would you like another drink?"

"No, thanks," Phoenix answered in his British accent. "This one's plenty."

"How about we split one?" Luna tried to entice him.

I walked up to Luna, who had now linked her arm with my boyfriend's.

"Where is Sebastian?" I said loudly. "I thought you two were inseparable. I remember you telling me all about your wedding. When is it, again?"

She shook her head. "There's no wedding," she retorted. "I mean, not now."

"That's okay. I was just leaving," Phoenix said.

"So soon?" Luna asked.

"I have some friends to meet at the Coffin Club," he said.

"Will you be back?" Luna asked, flashing her pink lashes.

"I might. With pretty girls like this one," he said, putting his hand to my chin, "it will be hard to keep me away."

Luna shot me a deadly gaze.

Phoenix put his drink on the bar and left the club through a maze of gawking girls. He could have had any girl in the Crypt; he was that magnetic. And I was one of those girls who was hypnotized. I wasn't sure when I'd ever see Phoenix again. At the last moment, I couldn't help but follow him out of the club. I knew he was not going to be returning anytime soon.

My heart was racing as fast as my feet. He was climbing on the bike when I caught up to him.

"Funny," I said. "Now that I know who you really are, I like you even better."

"Me, or Phoenix?" he asked.

"Both."

"Maybe now I can get that kiss that I didn't the last time?" he asked in his sexy British accent.

Phoenix stood up. His purple bangs hung over his forehead and gently brushed his eyes.

"It's okay. No one's looking," he reassured me. Phoenix drew me into him. "And don't worry, I won't tell."

I could feel his leather-clad legs against my naked knees.

He leaned in and gave me a long, deep kiss. It was so riveting I thought I'd lost all my wits. For a moment, I wasn't sure if I was kissing Phoenix or Alexander.

When we pulled apart I saw a figure lurking in the shadows.

Then I noticed blonde dreadlocks.

"Oh no!" I covered my mouth in shock.

"I better go." Phoenix revved up the motorcycle while I took off for the Crypt.

Sebastian gave me a death stare. His shoulders were tense and his face was fierce.

"Let me explain—" I started.

"I can't believe you—after all Alexander's done for you? And you do this to him?"

"It's not—"

"With some guy you've just met?"

"I already know him. It's not like you think. You don't even know what you're talking about."

"So you've been seeing him before—and that's your excuse?"

"I didn't mean—"

"So help me!" Sebastian was so hurt. I wanted desperately to tell him who Phoenix was, but if I did, the whole plan would be ruined.

"It's not what you think," I pleaded with him.

"What's there to think? You were making out with another guy and you're supposed to be in love with my best friend!"

"Please, Sebastian. Don't—you've misunderstood everything."

"No, I've only misunderstood one thing—you." He stepped past me and disappeared into the Crypt.

I felt as awful as if I had cheated on Alexander. Maybe the image was just as bad, if no one knew the truth.

I would have told Sebastian, but if he had loose lips, Alexander's cover as Phoenix would be blown. Even the events at the Coffin Club, where it was actually Alexander who prevailed at getting the vampire club to be civil, would now be known. And the worst part was that Jagger would feel betrayed and double-crossed and the truce would be broken.

That was something we couldn't afford.

I headed back into the Crypt. I tried to dance my feelings off on the dance floor. But when I saw Alexander's back sitting at the bar, next to Sebastian, I hurried over.

Sebastian didn't even turn around. I scooted next to Alexander.

"Sebastian hates me," I whispered in his ear. "He has lost all respect for me."

"He should. You were kissing someone else!" he said softly.

"Please, Alexander. It's not funny. We should tell him."

"But what if he spills it to Luna? I don't think we can take the chance."

"So this is how it will be?" I asked. "He'll go on thinking I'm cheating on you?"

"For the time being."

"I feel like Trevor," I mumbled, "but with a conscience."

"So, did you miss me?" Alexander said loud enough for Sebastian to hear. "What did you do until I arrived?"

Sebastian finally turned toward me. "Yes, Raven, what did you do?"

"I waited patiently for you to come," I said, giving Alexander a squeeze.

"Yes, that's exactly what she did," Sebastian said. "Waited by herself. All alone."

"Well, I was going to ask you to keep an eye on her, but you don't need to do that with Raven," he teased.

"I think you might want to start keeping an eye on her," Sebastian warned. "She isn't as patient as she looks."

18

T he next day Becky and I arrived at school to an unusual sight. Students were buzzing about the Crypt, and I noticed several girls wearing the same T-shirt Becky had given me for my birthday—black with THE CRYPT in white skeleton bone letters.

"That club rocks!" I heard the Prada-bee say to her friend. Her Crypt shirt was over her long-sleeve button down. "I can't wait to go again."

"I'm going every night," her friend retorted. She was wearing one, too, but it was underneath her green cashmere cardigan.

"How did they get those?" I asked Becky.

"I don't know," she said, just as bewildered as I was.

Several other students we passed as we headed to our lockers had Crypt shirts, but even those who didn't were blabbing about the fantastic time they had at the new club.

I was so pleased that even though I was still looked at as an oddball, we were all sharing in the same joy that was the Crypt.

Now that Alexander (as Phoenix) was key in cementing Jagger's mortals-only club policy, I breathed a sigh of relief knowing that my fellow students, family, and townspeople were in no immediate danger from unknown vampires. Maybe Scarlet, Onyx, and Sebastian would be staying in Dullsville. It would be a dream for me to spend time with them and Alexander in the darkened hours. Even Jagger and Luna, who were far from what I'd call best friends, could be a nice addition to this town. Jagger had made a fantasy of mine come true—and I had to give him major props for that.

And by the number of Crypt T-shirt–wearing students, Jagger could be next in line to my own nemesis, Trevor, in being Dullsville's most popular.

I opened my locker.

"Can you believe that tonight is finally your joint birthday party?" Becky said.

"I'm so excited, I can't wait. I wish we could just skip the school part and head straight to the club. But you know I wish that every day."

She laughed.

"But seriously, I can't even concentrate. I have a test third period and all I can think about are tombstones."

"What are you wearing?" Becky asked.

"I've tried on a million things. I can't decide between a minidress and a corset one."

"I can't believe that out of all the students, we get invites for the party. And you are the guest of honor," Becky gushed.

As we shut our locker doors, I walked proudly down the hallway, knowing I was going to open the Covenant just for us.

When we turned the corner, I bumped into Trevor, who was wearing a black Crypt T-shirt.

"Where did you get that?" I asked.

"I'm all out. Too bad I only have the one I'm wearing. Want to swap shirts? We can change here," he suggested with a wink.

"Thanks, but it would be best for all of us if you kept your shirt on."

The truth was Trevor had the best physique in school, but I wasn't about to tell him that. Besides, he already knew.

"So are you going to wear that special bracelet?" Trevor whispered as Becky got a quick drink at the water fountain.

I didn't say anything. My usual stinging barbs would have been funny but not totally appropriate. Trevor had given me a present—a real one. And to slam him would have made me a heel.

"Thank you," I said. "It was beautiful."

He was surprised at my sincerity.

I felt like hugging him. It was the right thing to do. I know he would have wanted a kiss, but I wasn't about to get sick to my stomach.

Trevor looked like he didn't know what to do. He was ready to slam me back, but since I had said something nice, he was speechless. He just grinned awkwardly and walked away.

"Hey, Trevor," I called.

"Yeah?" he asked, stopping. He stood with his hands on his hips, probably sure this time I was going to hurl a major verbal assault. He grinned like a champion.

I scurried up to him and before he could move, I hugged him. I hugged him so hard, I could feel his heart racing. For a moment I locked my hands together behind his back, like one hugging someone they really cared about would. I'd caught Trevor off guard.

He didn't know what to do. For a moment he didn't return my hug. Then he softened, as if he'd waited all his life for this display of affection. Just as he drew his arms around me, I stepped back.

Trevor smiled a bigger smile than I'd ever seen.

It was the least I could do. I was so excited about the party that even pressing my body against my nemesis to show my gratitude wasn't going to spoil it.

"Now I have to burn these clothes," I said to him as Becky caught up to me and I slipped inside my classroom.

Becky showed up at my house well before sunset. We modeled our outfits and tried out different hairstyles. She looked stellar in a black cami with a demi sweater and violet rayon skirt.

The doorbell rang as I was still trying to squeeze on my final outfit.

"They're here!" Becky said excitedly.

It wasn't like she never saw Matt. She saw him every day at school and on many evenings. But every time he arrived, she was just as thrilled as the time before. And I couldn't blame her. My heart pounded out of my chest every chance I got to see Alexander.

"Girls," my mom called from downstairs. "Your dates are here!"

I laced myself into my lavender monster boots, and Becky helped zip me into my black minidress and fix my barrettes. Since I'd gotten behind the time, I would have been a mess without her smoothing touches.

We descended the staircase like debutantes. Alexander and Matt were awaiting us, with huge smiles and in handsome club attire.

"Can I take a picture?" my mom asked.

"Mom!" I said, totally embarrassed. It wasn't enough that my boyfriend was a vampire and wouldn't even show up in the photo, but my mom making a fuss was more unbearable.

"Your dad is still at work," my mom said. "He'd hate to miss this moment."

"Oh yes, please, use my phone," Becky said. "I'll send you the pics."

I didn't even try to get out of it. Becky and Matt squeezed next to Alexander and me. We smiled as if Alexander were going to show up after all.

"Say cheese," my mom said.

Alexander squinted when the flash went off.

"Are you okay?" my mom asked.

"Just something in my eye. It was great seeing you, Mrs. Madison," Alexander said, giving my mom a polite kiss on the cheek. "Now our car awaits."

We gave quick hugs and good-byes to my mom as we walked out the front door and to the driveway, where Jameson was waiting with a limo.

"You are kidding me!" I screamed.

"Only the best for the best," Alexander said.

Becky and I continued to scream and giggle as we got in the back of the limo and headed to the Crypt like celebrities on their way to an awards show.

I arrived with my boyfriend and friends at the Crypt. I was excited to finally have the party celebrating Alexander's and my birthdays that Jagger had talked so much about. I wasn't sure what he had in store for us, but I knew it would be something special. The club was open to all its usual customers, but our party was going to be somewhere else in the club. I wasn't supposed to know the location, but I'd learned from Phoenix that we were finally going to see the Covenant after all.

We all milled about on the main floor until Jagger said it was time for the party. Becky approached me and seemed gravely concerned.

"What's up?" I asked. "It's party time."

"Nothing . . . it's just something that I've been weirded out by for a while."

"Did I do something?"

"No—it's not you. It's—"

"Tell me."

"I want to show you this," Becky said. She led me into an alcove away from dancing clubsters. She held out her phone. "Remember the picture I took at the soccer field again of Sebastian? He didn't show up in any of the pictures. He's clearly missing."

"That's all?" I asked. "Yes, that's weird. But maybe there is something wrong with your phone."

"I got to thinking. Maybe the rumor wasn't just a rumor."

"What do you mean?" I asked.

"All the signs. For so long now. I can't believe you—of all people—haven't noticed."

"What are you saying?" I asked my best friend.

"These are the pictures of the workers I took before Jagger told me not to take pictures." She showed me her phone again. There were no workers in view.

"Maybe they were out of the frame," I said.

"Everyone? All the pictures I took of you are perfect."

"Maybe it's time to buy a new cell phone. I think we have to get back—"

"And then this one." She took out a camera from her purse. "I used my camera this time. I took it tonight. It is of Jagger, Luna, and Sebastian."

"You weren't supposed to take pictures. . . ."

She held out the camera, shaking in her hand.

There wasn't anyone in the picture.

I didn't know what to say.

"Maybe it's the lighting?" I tried.

Becky's face was determined. "It's not the cell phone. It's not the camera. It's them!"

"Becky, you aren't making sense—"

"That's why Sebastian bit Luna at Alexander's party. That's why I've only seen them during the night and why they don't go to school. They can't. They are—"

"I have to get back—"

She reached into her purse again. "Then it won't matter if I throw these cloves of garlic on the dance floor."

I imagined it then. One by one, Alexander, Jagger, Luna, Sebastian, Onyx, and Scarlet breathing in the garlic fumes and gasping for breath. All laboring to get fresh air. Finally each one, falling to the floor. . . .

I reached for her purse. "No—you can't! You have to take that out of here! They won't be able to breathe!"

Becky was stunned by my reaction. Her face turned ghostly white. She pulled out an empty hand.

She could barely breathe herself. "Raven, I don't have any garlic. . . ."

I covered my mouth in horror.

"So it's true," she said faintly.

My best friend knew—about Jagger, Luna, Sebastian, Onyx, and Scarlet. And if I couldn't prove her wrong—or worse, lie to her—then it would be only moments before she realized the truth about Alexander, too.

My head swirled with excuses. The camera doesn't work, it's the lighting . . . but when I opened my mouth, no words came out. Instead I nodded, as if I'd been waiting for her to tell me those words forever. In fact, I must have been. She was my best friend and I'd kept the biggest secret from her—something I'd never done. And now she'd found out on her own, and I couldn't keep the secret any longer.

Her lower lip quivered and she wobbled in place.

"Becky?" I put my hand on her shoulder.

Becky began to succumb to her dizziness. Her knees buckled and she started to fall.

I quickly grabbed her with both hands, trying to keep her standing.

"What's wrong with her?" a clubster asked.

"She feels faint," I said. "Let's give her some air."

I held her up and guided her over to the bar, then helped her sit down.

"We need some water," I said.

I hugged my best friend. "It's okay, Becky. You'll be okay. We'll be okay."

The bartender put a glass of water on the bar.

"I'm not thirsty," she said, pushing it away.

"Drink it," I said, handing it to her.

Becky gulped it down.

For a moment we girls sat in silence, processing what had just happened. Becky had just learned my boyfriend's true identity and now I had to deal with my best friend holding this secret knowledge.

"I'm scared, Raven. I'm really scared."

Tears began streaming down her face. Her house of Hello Kitty cards was falling down in front of me. I was left breathless.

"And this picture, too," she said, scrolling her phone. "It's the one your mom took tonight with me and you and Matt and Alexander. Only Alexander isn't in the picture."

I couldn't speak nor look at the picture my friend was holding out, shaking in her fingers.

"So, does that mean—Alexander, too?"

I didn't answer.

"It's funny, really. I've never seen him in the daylight. Not once. And those pictures from the Snow Ball, he didn't turn out, and now tonight. . . ."

I nodded.

I knew she was frightened. For her, for me, for us. For the town. Even for Alexander.

"You tried to tell me once underneath the staircase at school. But I laughed at you."

"I would have laughed, too."

"Is it possible to be a good vampire?" Becky said.

"I think Alexander's proof."

Matt raced over. He noticed Becky's pale complexion. "What's wrong?"

"Becky feels faint," I said. "I think you should take her home."

"But they're going to have your celebration," she muttered.

"You've had enough for tonight," I said. "Matt, do you mind?" I asked. "I think she needs some rest."

"I don't want to leave," she said. "I want to stay. I want to know everything now."

"What do you want to know?" Matt said. "What is she talking about?"

"I want to know more about vampires," Becky said. "And Raven knows everything there is to know."

"Are you sure you're okay?" Matt asked.

Becky looked at me with a knowing smile. "I don't want to be left in the dark anymore."

I insisted Matt sit with Becky while she continued to drink her water and I went to find Alexander.

"I have to tell you something," I said when I finally found him by the club's entrance.

"It will have to wait. Jagger wants us to join him for the VIP party."

Jagger unlocked the Covenant door and waved us over. Becky and Matt trailed behind.

We walked down darkened, crooked wooden steps. When we reached the bottom we could clearly see the room Jagger had been hiding.

Twinkling tombstones lined the walls and morbid music played. "Happy birthday!" everyone cheered.

Sebastian, Luna, Scarlet, Onyx, Jagger, Trevor, and a few others who must have been friends of Jagger's from the Coffin Club applauded.

"And look at this. A covenant altar. Perfect for parties," Jagger said.

A wrought-iron, spooky spiderweb-designed trellis was beautiful. Underneath it lay a coffin with two antique pewter goblets adorned with bats.

"We are going to have a ceremony tonight. Just for

kicks," Sebastian said. "A mock ceremony to unite us with our girlfriends for eternity. I'm going first, then it's your turn."

"Are you kidding?" Alexander asked. "That is cool."

I kind of liked the idea. A mock covenant. Alexander and I could practice what it would really be like to have the ceremony and for me to be turned without it being a reality. Like posing for a picture with a wacky facade at a theme park. However, I'd be the only one in the picture.

Luna was dressed in a frilly taffeta pink dress and black monster boots. Her baby pink hair cascaded over her naked shoulders.

"Happy birthday, Raven," she said.

"Thanks, Luna."

"And happy birthday, Alexander." She stood on her tiptoes and gave him a peck on the cheek. "You'll soon find out what you've been missing," I heard her say.

"I can see why you're dying to have a covenant ceremony with Luna," I said to Sebastian. "She does look like an angel."

"She's a beauty," he said with a starry-eyed stare.

Becky came up to me and Alexander. She stared at him like she was seeing him for the first time.

She reached out to touch his arm as if she was trying to see if he was real.

"What's up?" Alexander said.

"Happy birthday," she said in a whisper. "But are you really eighteen?"

"Yes," he answered, confused.

"You're not really one hundred and eighteen?"

"No," Alexander insisted. "What are you talking about?"

She stepped back, then raced to Matt's side.

"What's wrong with her?" Alexander asked.

"That's what I've been trying to tell you. Becky found—"

Just then Jagger motioned us over to a giant cake sitting on a table. "Time to make a wish."

The cake was a long sheet cake with black flowers and tiny tombstones on it. In blood-red letters it read, "Happy Birthday, Alexander and Raven."

It was really sweet that Jagger had taken the time to decorate this room, get us this cake, and arrange for this party.

Two candles were burning like tiny torches.

Alexander and I looked at each other. We both made our separate wishes and blew out the candles.

"Thanks, Jagger," I said. I gave him a big hug. He was taken aback by my affection but seemed grateful for it.

We each took a piece of cake and then headed for the small dance floor.

"So it's just us?" Becky said. "Who are not . . . ?"

"You, me, Matt, and Trevor. But I still think Trevor is one, deep down," I teased.

"Scarlet and Onyx?"

"Oh yeah," I said as I danced.

"Are we in danger?"

"No—I carry garlic, just in case."

"You do?"

I shook my head. "You are safe tonight. Nothing is going to happen."

Just then Sebastian took a swig from a bottle. His mouth was stained with red liquid that he wiped off with the back of his hand.

"Is that wine?" Becky asked.

"I'm afraid not."

We continued to dance, and my friend tried to absorb her new reality without passing out.

It was then she spotted two marks on Luna's neck.

"I think I have to go to the bathroom," Becky said.

"Are you okay?" I asked.

"Yes," she said, starting for the door.

"I'll go with you," I said, and followed her up the stairs and into the girl's bathroom.

She splashed water on her face. "When did you know?" she asked.

"After Alexander's Welcome to the Neighborhood party. I was using Ruby's compact and he didn't show up in the reflection."

"That was months ago."

"I know."

"And you held this secret inside you for that long?"

"I had to. For everyone's sake."

"Who else knows?"

"No one. It's so important that no one else know."

"I'm not going to tell anyone. Who'd believe me? But I have to tell Matt."

"He'll have to swear to secrecy."

"He will," she assured me.

She dotted her face and neck with a paper towel. "I know this is a dream come true for you. But for me—"

"A nightmare?"

"Pretty much. Your boyfriend and all these people I've come to know are vampires."

"Can you believe it?"

"And they sleep here?"

"Yes, isn't that cool?" I said with a smile.

"In coffins?"

"Yes, you want to see?"

"You are joking."

"No, I'm not."

We left the restroom and I pushed through the crowd of clubsters, Becky trailing close behind.

"I'm not sure I'm ready for this," she said when we reached the spiral staircase. "I almost fainted once. And these stairs are spooky enough."

"It's just down here."

"Besides, don't you want to get back to the party? Matt is by himself."

"Alexander is with him." I'm not sure if that was comforting to Becky anymore. I, too, wanted to return to the party. I'd been waiting to celebrate for days, and in such a cool vampire way. But I'd also been waiting to share this secret with someone—anyone, especially my best friend—for so long now, it was comforting being able to reveal the load I'd been carrying alone.

"All right," I said. "I can show you later."

Just then Scarlet arrived behind us. "What are you girls up to?"

"Uh . . . I had to get something in Jagger's office," I said.

I didn't have to lie anymore, but I was so used to it, I wasn't sure what to say. Besides, I wasn't sure how Scarlet felt about Becky knowing she was a vampire.

"Cool. I have to go to our room, so we can walk together." She stepped around us and we followed her down the hall. "I just need to grab some fresh lipstick. Trevor rubbed it all off."

Becky hung back as Scarlet opened the door and popped inside.

"Do you guys mind if I take off?" Scarlet asked when she came back out. "I want to head back to the party. Sebastian and Luna are going to have their mock covenant ceremony. You don't want to miss it."

"We'll only be a sec," I said. "Are you feeling faint?" I said to Becky when Scarlet had gone.

"Sort of."

"Then we'll stop."

"I think this might be a dream," she said. "Hopefully I'll wake up any minute."

"Okay, but don't freak out if you don't." I opened the coffin room door wider so she could see in. There they were, five coffins in a row.

Becky screamed. Fortunately we were too far away from the Crypt for anyone to hear.

"That's how they sleep?" she asked.

"Yes."

"And Alexander, too?"

"His is black and it's at the Mansion."

Becky didn't move but remained fixed in the hallway. It was as if she expected one of the coffins to open and a dead person to jump out.

"No one is in them," I assured her. "They are all at the party."

"They really sleep here? Even Sebastian?" she wondered aloud.

"Yes, his is the one with stickers from different countries on it."

"A vampire was interested in me?" It was too much for her to take in on one night.

"Yes, he was."

"I feel woozy again."

She began to get weak-kneed, so I pulled her into Jagger's office.

"A tarantula?" she said nervously. "And gravestone etchings on the walls?"

"Maybe this wasn't the best place for you to sit down. But you should really catch your breath."

It was then I spotted the blueprints for the Covenant lying out on the table. On closer inspection I noticed something I hadn't seen before. These plans were old and weathered.

They were the original factory plans. In the margin, written in pencil, was a small area that remained untouched.

When I looked closer, it said, "tomb." Now I was ready to faint. It appeared to be a small burial site for soldiers. Part of the factory had been built over sacred ground—the part that Jagger now called the Covenant.

And any minute, Sebastian and Luna were going to have a real covenant ceremony. And unbeknownst to Alexander's best friend, it wasn't going to be "just for fun."

"Oh no!" I said.

"What?" Becky asked.

"We have to get upstairs!"

"I still feel woozy."

"Do you want me to leave you here?"

Becky recovered lightning fast. Before I could move, she was standing at the door.

I grabbed the original blueprints and we raced through the hallway and up the rickety spiral staircase. We squeezed through the crowd and scurried down the Covenant stairs.

When we reached the underground club, Sebastian and Luna were standing over a coffin on the covenant stage.

"Where were you?" Alexander said. "Sebastian and Luna are doing their ceremony. And we're next."

Trevor, Scarlet, Jagger, and Onyx were watching from the sidelines.

"I have to talk to you," I whispered.

"Shh!" Jagger scolded.

Sebastian held up a goblet and recited some words I couldn't understand.

"I have to talk to you—it can't wait any longer!"

"It will have to wait until after the ceremony," Alexander said.

Then Luna repeated the same words and took a drink from her goblet.

"We are on sacred ground," I said to Alexander.

"What?" he said.

Just then Sebastian turned to Luna. He held her hands and stared lovingly at her. He then took one hand and brushed her hair off of her neck. He smiled and leaned in.

I shoved the blueprints in front of Alexander and in my loudest voice declared, "We are on sacred ground!!!"

Sebastian stopped, and everyone in the club turned to me.

Alexander's face turned white, but it was Sebastian's face that was the most horrified. "What?"

I waved the blueprints. "We are over a real tomb. You are performing a real covenant ceremony!"

"I thought this was a joke. Just a game," Sebastian said, stepping back. He looked at Luna, whose bright face fell.

Sebastian jumped off the stage and shook his head. Disgusted, he pushed past us and headed up the stairs.

Jagger's face was red with anger.

Luna stood alone on the stage. It was the second time she'd been stood up at a covenant ceremony. First by Alexander, and now by Sebastian. Even I didn't wish that kind of rejection for her. I could see the horror and sadness in her face. One tiny pink tear fell down her porcelain white cheek.

"Luna—" I said, jumping up onstage to comfort her.

She gave me a killer stare that made me shudder. Then she stormed off the stage and out of the club.

Alexander went after Sebastian. Jagger was nowhere in sight.

Matt held Becky in his arms.

While everyone was in chaos, I took a moment at the altar. I imagined Alexander and me standing together over the coffin. He'd recite foreign words and lift his goblet and drink. Then I'd do the same. We'd face each other and stare into each other's eyes like a dream.

He'd take me in his arms and give me a lust-filled, passionate kiss, then slide his fangs up my shoulder until they met the nape of my neck.

"I've been waiting for this day for an eternity," he'd say.

Then he'd take the final plunge.

I sighed, imagining how happy I'd feel.

I spun around to find no one else in the room but Trevor, who was staring straight at me.

"My turn?" he said with a coy smile. "I can be into freaky foreign customs, too."

I grumbled and then stormed off the stage and out of the club.

So you think Trevor knows we're vampires?" Alexander asked the next day when I met him at the Mansion.

"No, he thought it was just something weird you guys do. But Becky knows the truth."

Alexander appeared worried. "Well, someone was bound to find out, I guess. It's funny. I came here to escape the Maxwells and now I've brought them to your town."

"You couldn't have known," I reassured him. "So is the feud back on?"

"It might be with Sebastian. But I think they were doing it to also get back at me."

Just then we heard a knock from downstairs.

"Alexander, you have a visitor," Jameson called. We headed out of the attic room and met Sebastian outside the TV room.

"Thanks, Raven. I owe you one." He leaned in and gave me a hug.

"I knew you liked her, but . . . ," I tried.

"So how are you doing?" Alexander asked.

"Pretty good," he said.

"What's going to happen to the Crypt?" I asked.

"It will remain open," Sebastian said, "but Jagger's losing a partner."

"Are you leaving town?" I asked, not able to mask the sadness in my voice.

"For the first time there is nowhere else I want to go," he said.

"Do you want to crash here?" Alexander asked.

"I don't want to mess with your setup," he said. "Besides, I need way more electricity than this Mansion can provide. I've found an apartment in town that's cool."

"You're staying?" I asked excitedly.

"Yeah, for a little while." He looked at his shoes as if he was trying to find the words. "I've always thought that Onyx was really pretty. And I don't like the way Jagger doesn't pay attention to her. She needs to know what a real boyfriend is like."

"And you're just the man?" I asked, thrilled.

"Who knows, I might be. Anyway, I just wanted to stop over and say thanks. I have to set up my new place. You guys can come over tonight if you want."

"That sounds great. I'll walk you out," Alexander offered.

While I waited for him to return, I heard Alexander's

phone beeping from the table. It beeped. And beeped.

If I wasn't calling him and neither was Sebastian, it might be his parents.

When I saw the caller ID, my heart sank.

Stormy.

Who was Stormy?

After a few moments of emotional flatlining, my blood pressure soared.

What do I do now?

I couldn't be that girlfriend—the kind who snoops in drawers and closets and invades emails and texts. Or could I?

When I saw the number's prefix, it was definitely foreign. Not from Dullsville or even the United States.

I looked at the message.

When are you coming back?

I miss you like crazy!

Luv,

Stormy.

Stormy! "Luv?"

My thoughts raced. Alexander had another girlfriend? It was the last thing I was intending to find. The number was foreign, so this girl obviously didn't live in Dullsville or even in this country. I hadn't imagined Alexander could be involved with someone else. Who was this "Stormy"? Was she pretty? Was she a vampire? And was Alexander in love with her, too?

I paced in my boyfriend's room. I gazed out the window. I tried to act calmly.

"That's cool that Sebastian will be staying in town,"

Alexander said when he reentered the room.

"Uh-huh," I said flatly.

"What's up?" he asked. "You seemed excited a few minutes ago."

"I am," I said indifferently.

"You seem weird. Distant. What's wrong?"

"Uh . . . nothing."

I'd imagined Alexander to be someone that maybe he wasn't. A guy who was straight and truthful. Who didn't have girls in every country. He was so handsome and wildly hot, I was a fool to think that girls wouldn't be throwing themselves at him.

I was wearing my broken heart on my black lace sleeve.

"Something's up," Alexander said. "I know that face."

"I just thought we were only seeing each other," I said, my voice cracking.

He was taken aback. "I am. Aren't you?" he asked, bewildered.

"I thought you weren't like other guys, like Trevor." My heart was aching.

"What are you talking about?" Alexander asked.

"Who's Stormy?" I asked. I handed him the phone.

Alexander paused. "You read my text?"

"The phone kept beeping and so I thought it might be something urgent. Something from your mother."

"Raven—" he said.

"Who's Stormy?" I demanded.

"She's my sister!"

I was floored. "What?" I said. "You have a sister?"

"Uh-huh."

"You have a sister?" I repeated.

"Yes. I have a little sister. Is that so terrible?"

"No! Well, yes, it is, because you never told me."

"You never asked," he said, half teasing. "And she never came up. I left my life suddenly when I came here to the Mansion. I didn't know how long I'd stay. I didn't plan on getting close to anyone here."

"But I've never even seen a picture. Or painting."

"Do you have a picture of Billy Boy in your room?"

"Uh . . . good point. But you've never even talked about her."

"I didn't think I'd be able to be close to anyone here—then I met you. And everything changed. But really, when we're together, I only want to talk about us."

If I didn't hear it straight from his dreamy lips, I'd have thought it was a line from a romantic movie.

"Honestly, talking about my family made me kind of miss them. So I never really did."

His voice was so sincere, I felt lonely for my boyfriend's situation. Here I was surrounded by my family, seeing them every day and celebrating my birthday with them. And Alexander lived in this big old Mansion alone.

I gave him a huge hug. First, I was sad for his plight, but second, I was so overjoyed that Alexander didn't have a secret lover. But he did have a secret sister. It was one of the reasons I loved him so much. He was so mysterious, and even after all these months I was still learning things about him.

"Do you have a dog, too?" I asked.

Alexander laughed. "A few pet bats."

"Stormy's lucky," I said. "She has the coolest big brother in the universe."

Alexander beamed at the compliment.

"I can see why she misses you. I'd hate it if I had a big brother and he left town for another country."

"She has full reign of the house. She's in heaven."

"I don't think so. Not with a brother like you. Stormy Sterling," I said. "It has an awesome ring to it."

"Her real name is Athena, but we call her Stormy."

"'A'—like Alexander."

He nodded.

"I bet she's really cool." Then it hit me. "She wants you to come home," I said.

"Yes," he said.

"So you'll have to go?" I said, my heart breaking again. "For a short visit? Or forever?"

"It would just be a short visit."

"I can't take that," I said selfishly. "We are already separated by the sunlight. Now by countries and weeks?"

"That's why I convinced her to come here."

"So you won't have to go?"

"No," he said, shaking his head.

"Then you'll still be here," I said, squeezing him with all my might. "And I'll get to meet her, too?"

"Don't be so excited. You'll have wished I had gone home to visit. We call her Stormy for a reason," he said.

And with that, Alexander turned off his phone.

Between creeps and Crypts, nemeses and best friends, pesky mortal families and visiting vampire parents and siblings, we were lucky enough to get any night time together. Alexander took this opportunity to lean in and flash his sexy fangs at me, and then led me into his closet room and opened his coffin and helped me inside.

He lowered the lid, closing the door on all worlds, mortal and immortal. He drew my hair back and rested his body next to mine. He pulled me in and kissed me with the heart and soul of a gorgeous, mysterious, and very romantic vampire.

Acknowledgments

To these fabulous people for their guidance in my career and support in my life:

Katherine Tegen, Ellen Levine, Sarah Shumway, and Dad, Mom, Mark, Ben, Jerry, Hatsy, Emily, Max, Linda, and Indigo